To my daughters, Katie and Savannah

Special Thanks
To Jimmy

With deepest appreciation and gratitude. Thank
you for everything and I appreciate all that you
do. Of my dreams that have come true, this one
is a favorite. I am very blessed because of you.

And to Al and June

The world could learn a lot from you both, and it's a better
place with the two of you in it. Thank you for touching
my spirit the way that you both have. If not for your love
of each other, I would not know the love I do now.

LILLIAN GRANT

TATE PUBLISHING
AND ENTERPRISES, LLC

Published by Tate Publishing & Enterprises, LLC
127 E. Trade Center Terrace | Mustang, Oklahoma 73064 USA
1.888.361.9473 | www.tatepublishing.com

Tate Publishing is committed to excellence in the publishing industry. The company reflects the philosophy established by the founders, based on Psalm 68:11,
"The Lord gave the word and great was the company of those who published it."

Book design copyright © 2016 by Tate Publishing, LLC. All rights reserved.
Cover design by Niño Carlo Suico
Interior design by Gram Telen

Published in the United States of America

ISBN: 978-1-68254-504-1
Fiction / General
16.01.21

Contents

Prologue

The sun was rising over the horizon of the ocean as it flowed past the jetties of the north tip of the island, its orange glow quickly turning to bright clear light. The cloudless sky was indicative of just how hot the day would be without them. In the salty sea breeze, I could smell a symphony of all the sweet aromas this island had to offer, played by an orchestra of orange blossoms and the gardens in full bloom. Great magnolias canopied paths of gardenias, roses, camellias, wisteria, and an assortment of all types of shrubbery—a floral euphoria. This was a small piece of what my idea of heaven on earth would be like. A place that was good for the soul just to sit and absorb it all, to reflect on days gone by and have wishful hopes for the future. I thought that if everyone could have a small special spot like this to go to, it would be a happier world we all lived in. I could sit here for hours mesmerized by my surroundings. Perfect clear skies and smooth seas always remind me of her. It was very much like this the morning she died. She used to sit in this same spot that I do now.

As beautiful as it was, it was a little less so these days without Caroline. And for the small part of the world she touched, it too had been touched by her. I may have been touched the most by her. She herself was touched. She called it her "inner eye" because that was what the generations before her had called it. I call it an intuition, something clairvoyant, almost oracular. She felt things, saw things that others could not. It was her gift, although not always a good one. I too have the gift. However, mine comes to me in my dreams. Until I came here, I didn't know what they meant. She taught me to understand them and to embrace their significance. There was always something to be learned from her. She was true to herself and never denied who or what she was. She was not always proud of her ancestors, but the patrimony left to her certainly had its rewards in possessing such a place as this. Caroline was the most genuine person I'd ever known. I'm fortunate to have known her, and I really wished I'd had more time to know her. For she is the reason I have all I do and the sole linkage to how my life is now. This had been the one opportunity that took me from losing everything I'd ever worked for to gaining even more back. I've built a great city out of the ashes within myself. All of it is with enormous thanks to her.

Caroline and my mother, Ruth, were cousins. I didn't have any memories of Caroline when I arrived here because I was too young to remember the last visit she had with my mother. But Caroline had fond ones of me as a very small boy. Occasionally, she'd recall an old memory and tell me about something I'd done that made her smile or laugh, none of which I can remember for myself. I wasn't familiar with this part of the family, nor did my mother ever discuss them with me. They had a falling out in which my mother never got over, and Caroline didn't seem to think it was such an issue that deserved never speaking again. I even tried one last time to find out more about the family while my mother lay in her deathbed. She wouldn't speak of them or of what happened then either. I only heard Caroline's side of it when I first came here. All the anger and bitterness my mother had stemmed from an argument over her not living up to her potential in Caroline's opinion, and she wanted my mother to do better for herself and her little boy. But she did things her own way. She didn't want to do better. She was happy with the way her life was. Whether or not anyone else was happy with her choices, she didn't care. My childhood could have been better if she had.

By the time Mom had passed, I was caught up in my own life. Although I hadn't a family of my own, I had a career as a police officer and working all the overtime I could get. I didn't have anything else going on, so I mostly just worked. And in a huge city like that, there is always work. Funerals, security for events at numerous venues, or just picking up an extra shift, there was plenty to keep the calendar full. And I've never been opposed to making an honest dollar. All my life I'd stayed out of trouble so I could serve on the force. I knew it was what I wanted to do since

I was eight years old. I made good grades and then went to college and earned my degree in Criminology. I made all the right choices to be were I was, and I'd worked so hard at it that I never for a moment thought it would be over in a flash. A split-second decision changed everything, and all I had ever worked for was gone. Everything. And it was only a matter of a few days after that split second that I needed security of my own—from "To Serve and Protect" to needing protection. It was, by far, the worst time in my life. I can't say for certain, but if it hadn't happened, I'm not sure I would be here.

There was no other choice but to resign when the grand jury refused to hand down an indictment to prosecute me for the death of that boy. The people were calling for my head to be served on a silver platter to the sheriff, and though it was a clean shooting, I couldn't even show myself in public. The media blitzed my face and name over every news station across the country. With headlines like "Officer Creed Lowe kills juvenile during racial profiling stop" and "Child Killer Cop," I didn't stand a chance in the city anymore. I figured it would turn into a life of hiding before it would all end. If it would ever end, I didn't know. At the time, my main concern was that if I wasn't indicted, the community would riot, which they did in a few small groups with the damage being minimal. The people never know the whole truth when something like that happens. They only know what the media tells them, and it's usually taken as gospel because some well-dressed news anchor said so. They inadvertently destroy people's lives reporting their stories, and as long as their hair stays in place and there aren't any glitches with the teleprompter, it's a good day for them, regardless of the lives they ruin.

Most of the public never learned the full story. They didn't know he was stopped because we were already looking for him. There were witnesses and video surveillance to the bludgeoning death of a homeless man that he participated in earlier that day, laughing as they ran away. Then he attacked the officer that stopped him and managed to get his gun away from him while wrestling him to the ground, never obeying my commands to stop. When he kneeled over and pointed the gun at the officer, I got two shots off before he could kill the officer. That kid was sixteen years old and already six feet, six inches tall and 270 pounds. He was quite a lot bigger than the officer he aimed to kill, and clearly he used his size to his advantage in getting him down to the ground. It was never reported that he didn't attend school because he'd been expelled for beating a teacher unconscious or that he had a record already and on probation for several robberies and assaults in his neighborhood. All the public ever heard was how he came from a broken home, was fatherless, had a prostitute mother strung out on meth, and being raised on welfare. He was made to be an innocent child, which he wasn't, and I was presented to the world as a trigger-happy, racial profiling baby killer.

My future was looking very bleak. There wasn't anywhere I could live and not be recognized. And where would I work? I couldn't have even got a job as a security guard at the mall. It was, without a doubt, the worst time for me, but it turned out to be perfect timing on Caroline's part. I accepted her offer to come here to Twisted Oaks for a number of reasons. Primarily because I thought it would be safe, and I could live in peace. I could still earn a living and be away from the rest of the world while getting to know this part of the family that was hidden from me most of my life.

What else was I going to do? It wasn't as though I had a list of doable options, and even if I did, I'm sure this would still have been the one I'd have chosen. However, I was concerned about the adjustment. I spent my entire life until that point in the big city, and I wasn't sure how it was going to go. Even with all the issues that came along with it, I'm happy I ended up here. All I have is because of her. She was the catalyst at that pivotal moment in my life, and I will be eternally grateful to her for it.

As I sat on the wooden bench swing her husband, Luke, crafted for her just before their third wedding anniversary, my thoughts were with her. He built it facing east so they could watch the sunrise together, as I do now. I wondered if she was with her beloved Luke, somewhere on the other side—in that place she talked about. He died a few years before my arrival, and although we never met, I feel like I knew him. She told me so much about him, and she said I would've liked him. Everyone liked him. Caroline missed him terribly, and I really believe what she really died from was a broken heart. Doc told me a person can't die from a broken heart, but I think she did, and I often thought that the memories of her loved ones are what kept her soul alive. Luke was the only man who accepted her for just the way she was. He loved everything about her, including all of her faults and shortcomings, and her gift didn't bother him at all. She was the only woman he had ever been with due to his convictions and the only one he would ever love. Being the man he was is what made her love him just as much as he did her. She always kept his spirit alive, never doubting she would be back in his arms someday. Even if it was only on some celestial plane and not in their ideal heaven, she didn't really care as long as she could be with him again.

In a way, I understood that. Having a wife of my own now, I don't ever want to be without her either. And when our time comes, I hope to see her again wherever that is. She too is everything to me as Luke and Caroline were to each other. I can't fathom my life without her since she became a part of it. I didn't know she would have the fervent effect that she did on my life, and life without her would be unbearable. I wouldn't change any of it, except to bring Caroline back if I could. Megan is probably the best of all that's happened. She is a fine woman with good morals and fortunate enough not to have any of the haunting gifts bestowed upon this family. Sometimes when the dreams come and she says she wishes she had the gift so it would help her better understand them for my sake, I tease her by telling her I'm glad she didn't because then that intuition may have told her to stay away from me. She always smiles and says that even wild horses couldn't drag her away from me. And I always think how permanent death is. I'll have to wait for her no matter which of us goes first. And I really hope Caroline is right about her beliefs in the afterlife. I'd love nothing more than forever with my adoring wife.

I hope there is a forever. I am a believer, but that doesn't mean I'm right. Megan thinks there's a heaven, and I like to think that she's right and that her faith alone could create one, even if there isn't. She was raised by Luke and Caroline after her mother died, so it's no surprise she believes that. But what if she's wrong? Do we then just rot? No, there has to be something. I can't honestly think for one minute that there is nothing. But if there isn't anything, I will leave this world knowing I had everything. More than money, health, or good times, I had her. I had Megan's love, and she's the woman made just for me. And to have her in life is worth an eternity of dark emptiness if she is wrong about that heaven she so deeply believes in. Death is imminent for us all, but for now, I'll take the not so permanent with her. She is everything to me, and for whatever reasons, she seems to feel the same about me.

She loves me like Caroline loved Luke. If everyone loved the way they did, people would be so much happier and the world would be a wonderful place.

Happy is feeling real love and knowing that they are deeply loved too and that the person they love so much loves them just as deep. It's a beautiful thing. The world would be so wonderful. Wonderful, the way humans would be if they actually treated one another with respect and decency. The effect on humanity would be profound. Great things could come from such kindness toward our fellowman, but by nature alone we are eager to watch the next man fail. It makes those that are this way feel better about themselves. Human nature sometimes can't be avoided simply because it's what we are. But sitting here on this glorious morning, it's as though the rest of the world doesn't exist. I know it's out there somewhere, but here it seems like we are the only ones on the planet. And I like it that way.

The fortune I've acquired has also helped, to say the least. When does it not? It's good not to worry about such things when I have enough on my plate to worry about. Caroline told me that if I accepted her offer, I'd be a wealthy man in a few years, and she was right. I've earned a fortune and have amassed enough that my future generations will have plenty. Although money can't buy you happiness, it can sure make you comfortable. It's a comfort to not be concerned with having the money to pay the bills when they come due. It allows me to handle the other things that have to be dealt with in a place such as this. And the dreams. But mostly, I need to keep a clear mind and a level head for this job. Sometimes the decisions have to come quick, and the less I worry about one thing, the better I can focus on another. And here I must have focus. Things can happen so fast, and forced change strikes like lightning that either you recover from the shock or die from it. It could drive a person to madness in such a place as this, so far from civilization and the world as most people know it. Out here, we have to handle things on our own. We take care of what we have to by ourselves for the most part. Occasionally, there is a need to seek outside help, but I haven't needed to yet.

Hopefully it won't ever be necessary. So far we have managed on our own. I intend to keep it that way.

I had no way of knowing, of course, just how profitable this island was until I saw my bank account explode. I soon realized the grove to be a valcano of wealth that erupted every year at harvest. Its lava flowed in the form of delicious Amber sweet oranges, the finest in the world grown right here for the elite that can afford them. Kings and presidents pleasure in their super sweet juiciness and tender texture for juicing—we send them to the far corners of the world for those who don't mind the price. The price was set by the standard of the oranges themselves and as to how many are estimated to be harvested for our season. Since they are only available once a year and the demand is so high, most of the crop has reservations set by particular buyers before the blossoms have fully set for the year. We always meet our order demands and have enough for ourselves as well. Caroline thought it was a combination of the nitrogen rich soil, the fresh water spring, salt air, and the viciously hot summers that made them so good. Whatever it was, the trees were always free of rust mites and canker. It was as though the trees were immune to parasites and disease. It seemed like everything is like that here—immune to most of the bad things that destroy. Not all bad things, but most.

It isn't just the oranges that are profitable but the honey and the bees too. The bee shortage is a worldwide problem, and the bee population is three times greater here, and queens are nine times higher in ratio to standard reproduction statistics, so we send hives to different parts of the world that have bee population reductions to help replenish their bees and help maintain their ecosystem. No one knows why the bees are in greater numbers here or why they do so well, even living two days longer than other honeybees. It's one more thing that makes this place so special. And the honey they made from the orange blossoms is perfectly sweet with a smooth caramel copper color. It goes good on anything, and we never run out, always keeping more than enough in our own reserves. There is very good money to be made in hive and honey sales, and it's far more than the oranges alone.

And running things around here is no simple task. There is a lot of work that goes into keeping order, and order is kept by everyone here. However, on occasion, things can get out of hand, situations become heated, and this is where I step in and the solution is resolved by my final decision in any situation that cannot be resolved otherwise. Most of the time, all is well, but there are those moments when duty calls for me to have the last say. Sometimes while confiding in Megan, she will say,"Heavy is the head that wears the crown."She has a way of saying things and putting things in a different perspective, and that makes things easy to grasp and understand particular things that I may see one-sided. It is like being king when you control most everything. This was like a kingdom, and some days that crown is heavy, but most days it's just good to be king. I think of Caroline and the way she seemed to be the queen of all things. She made good decisions for her kingdom, and I hope to carry on her legacy in the same manner she would have. Do what is best for everyone, even when it's not what I want to do, for the greater good of everybody here like she said. I still have moments when I wonder what Caroline would do or how she would have handled some matters at hand. She always knew the answers, even when it wasn't the answer she wanted. She made the right decisions, and she was right about everything.

Caroline was especially right about what wealth is. It wasn't just what the balance is in the bank or the property one may hold. Wealth is many things. It's knowledge and what we do with that knowledge. It is family and the ones we love—not family in the fundamental sense but in the chosen sense. Caroline believed that we cannot pick who we are born to or who other members of one's family are, that these are the fundamental relationships in which we cannot choose. More importantly, the chosen relationships in which we chose to be a part of someone else's life are generally the most endearing and rewarding. As much as blood meant to her, it was the family that wasn't blood-related that were the most precious to her. The most challenging of her relationships were always the family. They gave her the most grief, which does explain why she felt the way she did about some of them. But she loved them nonetheless, in spite of their differences. Differences that were, quite often, extreme.

My prosperity was beyond measure in that I had my own family now. More than knowledge alone and more than money, I have created my own bloodline, my own lineage with my very gifted and beautiful wife. They too will grow up here like their mother, surrounded by all the splendor that nature has to offer on this island. They will learn the things they wouldn't be able to learn anywhere else. I suppose they won't have dozens of friends like other children from the city or ones that attend county schools, but they also won't be exposed to the dangerous sects of society either. It's one less worry. I consider this to be a good thing, though not everyone would agree. My eldest daughter has Caroline's gift, while my youngest has his mother's. When I look into her eyes, I see it, and in a way, I think it's better than having the dreams. Although I don't know how the clairvoyants share their works, I do hope that if she ever has trouble understanding it, I can be there to help her as Caroline helped me with the dreams. Some of them being so daunting and unnerving without knowing what they meant was, at times, maddening and taxing to my psyche. She helped me with so much. I owe her everything for all I am today. I hope she knew how grateful I am and that I am indebted to her until I die.

Caroline told me once that we had to appreciate all we had. No matter what we had or who we were, we still had to be happy for what we had.

Good and bad, it made no difference. Even if we were destitute, we had to be thankful for it. She said we are supposed to learn from life's downfalls and pick ourselves up out of whatever mess we have gotten ourselves into. I remember she would say,"You wouldn't appreciate the good if you never had the bad."This is true. I wonder if I would know the difference if there was never any bad to compare to the good if I would know what good really is. I do know this; absorbing all she has taught me hasn't been easy. Some lessons came with great difficulty, while others did not, and all the while learning and taking it all in. I can't say I agreed with all of her beliefs or shared all of the same thoughts, but in talking with her, she could definitely make me see where she was coming from. I truly miss her and our talks, and I guess I always will. Sometimes I think she is still here, lingering around to make sure I'm doing a good job and taking care of everyone like the good man she wanted me to be, the good man she knew I would be.

It hasn't been the same without having her to turn to, but I make due because I have to, I need to. I'd like nothing more than to meet everybody's expectations of me. I don't always, but I do my best. There are times I talk to her when nobody is around, and I like thinking she actually hears me. Sometimes I almost hear her replies in the gust of wind that comes after I've spoken to her. I thought I heard her calling for me this past week, and then when I turned around, there was no one there, just me standing there alone. That would disturb most people, but for me, it's comforting. It's sort of the norm. What isn't normal for the rest of the world is everyday normalcy here. What others wouldn't understand, we do, and we all accept it because it's the way it is. It's how we maintain and keep our sanity by acceptance. Although there are particular things that are hard to digest, I've done fairly well in doing so, especially without her guidance. I believe Caroline would be happy for me, and I hope she is happy too. One can only guess.

To be in this very spot she once called hers, with the warm sea breeze in my face, is one of my favorite things to do, and every day here is special to me. Sitting here by myself is the best way to assimilate the past, take it in, absorb it all, and sort it out. Usually, no one comes from the house when they see me out here. They all figure I'm contemplating what decisions need to be made, and sometimes I am, but not today. Today my thoughts are primarily of her and all she's done. Maybe the world isn't a better place because of her, but this small part of the world most certainly is, and I'm a better man for it. The blood we share is thin, but it felt thicker than any other, including my own mother.

In my darkest hour, she shined through like the beacon from a lighthouse for the ship that is lost in the night. She turned that pivotal moment into the pinnacle of my life. So much good has come from the bad that if those bad things had not happened, the good ones would not have happened either. I wouldn't be here; I'd still be there in my old life. That thought reminds me of her words,"Everything we do, every decision we make, brings us to this very moment right here and now. It's what we decide to do with this moment that makes us who we are. Those decisions made yesterday define who we are today, and today's decisions will define who we are tomorrow."And what followed made just as much sense to me,"Make all your choices very carefully, Creed, because freewill and karma go hand-in-hand. Where one goes, the other will soon follow."And so it does.

Out of the Darkness

Creed sat on the side of the king-sized bed in the suite of his current hotel, which served as his temporary residence, and washed down two of his little blue pills with a few swallows of cheap whiskey. They were supposed to calm his nerves, but for him, they just took off a little of the edge. He picked up his Smith & Wesson revolver from the side table and held it in his lap. Looking at it, he thought about doing it. It could all be over in a nanosecond if he really wanted it to be, but deep down, that wasn't what he wanted, and he knew that the press would be all over it. After everything that happened, he wasn't going to let the vultures have another word to say about him, especially something such as his suicide. They would love to report that story. Creed wasn't about to give them or the people who held rallies in protest of the outcome any such satisfaction no matter how much anguish he lived with. So he put the gun back down on the table and took a deep breath and then let out long sigh.

The devil hates a coward, he thought. As much as it seemed that the situation wasn't going to get better, he hoped it would. His emotions and thoughts had been eating him alive for a while, and sometimes he wasn't sure how he was making it from one day to the next. All he really knew was that he was still aboveground and breathing.

After some thought, he decided he would get a shower and something to eat. Although he wasn't very hungry, he knew he, at least, had to eat. As he stood to head for the bathroom, he noticed the light on the phone beside the bed was flashing. He turned the ringer all the way down the night before, so he wouldn't be bothered. Its red dome bulb almost sparkled with each blink, making him aware he had a message and should contact the front desk. Only being at this one for a couple of days, he wondered who would know he was here and, more importantly, what they wanted. Maybe a reporter found out where he was or, perhaps, another of the numerous death threats. He was in no mood for either. Hopefully it would be to see if he wanted housekeeping or some extra towels. He decided against it and opted for the shower instead. He was hoping the meds would have kicked in by the time he dried off and he would be in a better frame of mind to call the front desk. If it had been someone in the lobby to see him, he hoped he could wait them out with a shower and they may go away. Besides, the hot water running down his back always helped clear the fog in his head.

As usual, the hot water trick worked its magic, and Creed was actually starting to feel better when the banging on his door started. *Can't a man take a shower in peace?* he thought. Creed had come to the realization that there really was no rest for the weary. He shut the water off, grabbed one of the plush white towels, and began drying himself when another series of the distinctive rapping on his door started again. He yelled out, "Just a minute!" in no hurry to answer. By the tempo, he knew it was just Otis anyway. He wrapped the towel around his waist, tucked it in, and headed for the door. *Geez, what's the big deal?* he thought, wiping a few missed water drops on his arm. As he opened the door, it was Gerald instead. Otis and Gerald Montgomery were identical twins who were assigned to Creed's security team. It didn't take long for Creed to learn the difference. Although both men were huge, Gerald was slightly smaller.

"I was in the shower, Gerald. Where's the fire?" he asked the colossal man.

"No fire, Mr. Lowe. You have a message from the front desk. They tried to call, but you didn't pick up, so they brought it up to your room. The girl that gave it to me said it's important."

Creed took the envelope from Gerald's outreached hand. "Thanks and please call me Creed," he replied.

"Yes, sir, Mr. Lowe. If you need anything, I'll be right out here," said the mammoth.

"I know. Thanks again."

Creed sat at the foot of the bed and admired the petite envelope. He found it interesting in that it was embossed with what looked to Creed like a land mass shaped similarly to a kidney bean with an orange blossom-shaped overlay. "That's odd," he said to himself. "I've never seen anything like this. That's a pretty unique stationery. It must be an invitation to the ball." Then he laughed out loud. *Who would send me something here?* he wondered. Furthermore, why did Gerald accept it? No one could have known where he was already. He flipped the envelope over and noticed the orange wax stamped seal on the back flap. This ignited his curiosity even more. Eager to see what was inside, he quickly tore it open by its seal. He pulled out a folded piece of note paper with the same imprint as the envelope and read it. It was simply a name and a phone number. It read:

> Ray Nussbaum
> Emissary for Caroline Louder
> 904-305-1119
> Your Call Will Be Expected

Why that name seemed so familiar was puzzling, almost troubling, him. *How do I know that name?* he thought. As he sat in bewilderment, he just couldn't place it. "Who is she?" he said. Even more worrisome was what did she want with him? Creed thought he'd ask Gerald, maybe he had heard of her. He went to the door, opened it, and poked his head out into the hallway.

Gerald, as faithful as he was, responded immediately, "Everything all right, sir?"

"Um, yes, I was wondering if you've ever heard of someone named Caroline Louder?"

Gerald's brow peaked, and he looked both ways down the hall before answering, "I can't say I have, sir. But maybe you should find out if that's who sent the message."

Then Creed asked, "What about Ray Nussbaum? Ever heard of him?"

Again, Gerald replied, "I can't say I have."

"Okay, thanks anyway." Creed shut the door back and went to have a seat by the phone. He thought about how strange the message was and if he should be in a rush to make that call. After giving it some thought, he figured it might be best to get it over with and see what they wanted. The worst that could happen is he would have to move to a different hotel. "No time like the present," he proclaimed, and then he picked up the phone's receiver and began dialing.

The other end rang just twice, and then a hearty voice answered, "Hello, I'm happy your call has come. I was hoping it wouldn't take too long."

Creed was surprised that the man had a notion of who was calling and asked, "Is this Ray Nussbaum speaking?"

The man at the other end said, "It is. The one and only, and you are Creed Lowe."

Creed said, "Yes, I am. I have a message to call you. Now I'm inquisitive as to why."

Ray snickered a little and then said, "I'm sure you are, so I'll get to the point."

"Please, by all means," Creed anxiously replied with a hint of sarcasm. He certainly was in no mood to discuss anything, but trying to figure out the name was gnawing at him. He could endure the senseless chatter long enough to solve the mystery as to who this Caroline was and why she had a need to send a representative on her behalf.

"In that case, let's not waste any time. We've done enough of that already," Ray said, but before he could continue, Creed interrupted.

"What the hell does mean?"

The stranger paused for a moment and then said, "I didn't mean to offend you, but there are other matters at hand that need your attention as well. I meant no disrespect. What I meant was that you could be doing better things than bouncing from one hotel room to the next, having to hide from the rest of the world. You're needed elsewhere," the stranger answered.

"Like what? Where could I possibly be needed? What is this about? And who are you anyway?" Creed began to demand.

"Slow down there, one question at a time. Just let me explain, and it may answer most of what you're asking. I'm here by Mrs. Louder's authority to offer you an opportunity for work and at the same time escape your current situation.

She understands your life has been turned upside down, and she would like to help you." Ray explained.

Creed didn't understand yet what was happening, but he was curious to know more, and the man on the other end of the line hadn't quite answered all the questions he had.

"What kind of work? And who is Mrs. Louder?" were the next of questions from a list in Creed's mind that was getting increasingly longer by the second.

"It would be a combination of things but mostly security. You know, um, to help keep order when needed, which isn't often. And apparently you don't remember Caroline Louder, but she was the one that awarded you that fat scholarship for college." Ray informed him. "Do you remember her now?"

There was a long silent pause as Creed processed what Ray said. Creed had forgotten her name, and that was the good reason it seemed familiar. He won the scholarship for an essay he'd written his senior year of high school about why he wanted to become a police officer and how he could serve his community best by doing so. To his surprise, he won first prize that was a full scholarship to any college of his choice as long as he majored in Criminology. For a moment, he actually felt guilty for not remembering her name. After all, he paid almost nothing himself while in college. His books, housing, and meals were all paid for by the scholarship fund. He could've, at least, remembered who awarded him the nicely furnished apartment with a twenty-five-hundred-dollar-a-month allowance for all the other necessities a young man needs. He felt his heart sink as he said to Ray, "Yes, I recognize the name now. I sent her a thank-you card with a letter of appreciation for all the help. I couldn't have gone to college had it not been for her endowment, so, yes, I do remember now. And I'm sorry I didn't recall who she is sooner."

"It's okay, you've been through a lot lately. You really don't know who she is, do you?" Ray asked.

"I just told you. What do you mean?" Creed replied. Again, there was a long pause before Ray answered.

"Caroline's maiden name is Lenoit, Caroline Lenoit. Does that one ring a bell?"

Creed did know this name. Although he knew the name, he wasn't sure which of his kin she was, but he did know this was a family name from a limb somewhere in the tree that his mother never spoke about. His curiosity at its summit yet, he suddenly felt lost and confused. All along, she was family, and he hadn't known. He wondered why she hadn't tried to contact him or tell him who she was.

"Yes, I know of her. I believe she is a relative of mine. But to be perfectly honest, I'm not sure which one," Creed answered, more befuddled than ever as to what was going on.

"She knew you probably wouldn't. Your mother, Ruth, didn't associate much with the family. Anyway, Caroline and Ruth were cousins. You'll have to get the rest from Caroline yourself." Ray explained.

Then Creed asked in a solemn tone, "So why didn't she contact me directly instead of you?"

"She tried, but you don't answer your phone these days."

This was true. Since his perils began a couple of months prior, he had stopped answering altogether, and after the death threats started, he'd stopped checking his voicemail as well. Lately he didn't even check his missed call log either.

"Yeah, I'm sorry about that. I haven't kept up with it recently."

"We know, that's why I'm here, Creed." Ray started to explain.

"Caroline would like to extend an invitation for you to come out and hear what she would like to offer you."

Creed didn't know why she would want to offer him anything. She didn't really know him, but at the same time, he did have a desire to learn more about his heritage that was such a mystery to him. Maybe, he thought, this could be a good chance to do so. What else did he have to do but to keep running from place to place? He might get a break if he got away from everything. He was thinking about it for a moment when he heard Ray.

"Hello, are you still there?"

"Yes," Creed said, snapping back into the conversation. "Yes, I'm still here, Mr. Nussbaum. I was just thinking."

"Please, call me Ray. And what are you thinking?" Ray asked.

"Actually, I was thinking that it's not a bad idea," Creed said to his own surprise.

"So can I let her know you've agreed to come out?" Ray asked, happy that Creed had made the decision so quickly.

Creed replied, "I suppose so, but where is out? Where should I go to meet with her and when?"

Ray was delighted to tell Creed anything he wanted to know. He was not only Caroline's delegate but also her best friend and closest confidant. He couldn't wait to share the news that Creed had agreed to come. It was something she had wanted for a long while, but that she hadn't felt to be the right time until his recent setback. He knew this was going to please her, and that was something she needed right now.

"It's an island called Twisted Oaks, and if you could be available in the morning, I'll take you there. You would need to stay over for the night, and I could bring you back the following evening if that would work for you," Ray responded.

"An island? Well, why would I need to stay over?" Creed inquired, thinking how odd of a request it was. Not that he had anything more pressing to do than to dodge the reporters and paparazzi.

"Because it's a big place and there is a lot to go over, not to mention, I'm sure you two would like to catch up, wouldn't you? I know she would," Ray answered.

Creed thought about what the man said and figured he was probably right. Since he had not met her, it would be good to spend a day and night learning about that side of the family that he never got the chance to know. Besides, it was an island. It would be nice to visit such a place. Not once in his life did he ever set foot on an island. He had been on plenty of boats, but none had an island destination.

"Yes, actually, I would like that. Where should we meet and what time?" Creed asked.

Then Ray replied, "Do you know where Harlen Marina is?"

"I think so. Isn't that the one past Hope Landing?" he asked him.

"That's the one. I'm docked in number sixteen. Can you be down there in the morning by eight?" Ray asked.

"Sure, I'll be there," Creed said.

Like a kid on Christmas day, Ray nearly squealed with excitement. "That's great, Creed. I'm really looking forward to it. I can't wait to let her know you'll be coming. Would you rather that I pick you up at your hotel?"

Creed thought about it and then declined. "That won't be necessary. I'll just meet you there."

"Okay, well, I'll see you then. Thank you and I really appreciate you returning my call," Ray said.

Creed declared quickly, "No, thank you. I appreciate the call. And if you wouldn't mind, would you pass the same along to Caroline? Let her know I'm looking forward to meeting her."

"I'll do that with great pleasure. I always like putting a smile on her face, and this will definitely do it," Ray replied.

"Okay, have a good evening, and I'll see you tomorrow. Good-bye and thanks again," Creed said. Then he set the receiver down in its cradle. He sat there for a few minutes, pondering over what just occurred. He couldn't believe he'd had such a conversation or that he was going to get the chance to meet other relatives he hadn't met before. For the first time in a while, he felt some encouragement that this wasn't the end of his life. He had something to do besides hide in a room. The worst case scenario: he'd decline the offer and come back here. But for now, he had a glimmer of hope, and that was a very good feeling. He noticed a slight smile had eased itself upon his face, and for the first time in a long time, he did feel good. It was almost new, in the sense that most outlets of his life had become negative, and to have, even for a brief moment, a little bit of positive was a very good thing. He would take all the positive he could get, especially right now.

Later on that day, Creed kicked his shoes off and leaned back against the large fluffy pillows he had piled up earlier. He decided he would rather stay in, so he ordered a cheeseburger with French fries and a couple of sodas from room service. He didn't usually eat that kind of stuff. He was no doughnut cop for the most part; he ate right and tried to take care of himself until that calamitous day when his life fell apart. "Life is all a blunder" is how Creed termed it. That was when the nerve pills and drinking started. His run with those two had been short, but dependency for them came hard and swift. He knew it, and he was using less in an attempt to wean himself off both of them. It was the last thing he needed, and he was trying to work on it, just short of rehab. That he really didn't need. He thought that if he was tied up with Caroline, he may not think about his habit, and that might help too. He would be busy talking with her, seeing about her offer and hopefully getting some information about the family he knew so little about. The more he thought about it, the more he wanted to know.

As he lay there, he soon thought of all the things he should have asked the stranger who answered his call, like where was this island? And who is Caroline Louder that she could send someone to do her bidding? It seems she must be of importance and affluence if she can do that. He knew she had a foundation named for her because of the tuition grants and financial backing that put him through school, but other than that, he really didn't know anything else. Then to top it all off, he happened to be related to her. His mind was racing, and his stomach was growling.

He sat up from the bed and reached for his laptop, which had been charging on the other bedside table. He thought he'd look up what he could online about the woman with whom he would be second cousins with and of the island for which Ray called Twisted Oaks. Then he thought about that stationery again. Who does that anymore with the wax stamp and with the land mass imprinted on it? He now assumed this was the island they spoke of on the phone. What else would it be? Another of the many questions his mind was making list of.

Before he could start his research, there was that rhythmic beat on the door that Creed had grown accustomed to. He opened the door, and there Gerald stood, keeping the porter delivering his meal from getting close to the door. As Creed opened it, it dawned on him that he neglected to tell his guard that he was getting food.

"I'm sorry, Gerald. I forgot to tell you that I ordered something to eat."

Gerald nodded his head and stepped to the side to let the covered platter held by a very nervous, sheepish teenage kid, probably working through the summer to save money for something special, pass. Creed took the tray and handed him a folded-up five-dollar bill.

The young man took it and then walked away hurriedly. Creed looked at Gerald, shook his head, and said, "Just trying to eat here, big fella, okay?" Gerald nodded his head again, and Creed closed the door. He set his dinner down and moved his laptop to the desk in his suite. Two birds, one stone. He could eat and do some studying at the same time. What else did he have to do? He thought he would look up Caroline Lenoit Louder first. That way he could find out the most about her before he checked out that place, Twisted Oaks.

He uncovered his tray and inhaled the delicious aroma of his cheeseburger. He was hungrier than he thought he was and took three big bites, realizing that he hadn't eaten since the previous day. It was no wonder he was starved, he thought. He surely didn't wake up hungry. As he scarfed down some fries, he typed in what he wanted from the web beginning with a biography of her. But he soon discovered there was no such information on her. All he could really get was that there was a foundation named for her that adopted out orphaned children that the state wasn't having any luck with. And from what he read, every child that had come through the foundation had been placed with a good, loving home, eventually being adopted by their new families. Creed was curious as to how they could get them all a home and why he'd never heard of them. After all, there were many times as an officer he was called to a home and the children had to be removed, and a representative from Children's Services with the state would have to come and get them. It was always a sad thing for everyone involved.

Other than the foundation naming, he couldn't find anything else about her. He found this to be odd considering most anything can be found out about a person these days. Information about everyone is out there waiting to be turned up when looking in the right places. But not on her; he researched for nearly two hours and nothing. Then he tried "Twisted Oaks Island," and again nothing. How could it be that he couldn't find a thing, no history, no maps? Unless, he thought, it didn't exist. He wasn't sure what to think; it didn't make any sense, but he knew he would have to discuss all of this further with the Ray Nussbaum fella before he leaves the mainland with the stranger who claims to be here on said family's behalf. The list of questions in his mind had grown into dozens, and his head began to ache. He thought it would be best not to dwell on it too much since the throbbing in his skull had started. It was going on nine fifteen, and he decided he'd be better off to go to bed and try to get some rest, at least, if he couldn't get actual sleep.

However, there was one last order of business before that would happen. He still needed to let his security team know that he would need to be going out. He didn't want to forget that again since it could be a problem without the proper notice. He got up and went for the door, not knowing which of them would be out there this time. When he opened it, there was Otis.

"Good evenin', sir," the hulky man blurted out before Creed could utter a sound. Not only was he slightly larger than the twin, who stood duty a little earlier, but his personality too was larger than life.

"Yeah, hey, Otis, how's it going?" Creed asked.

"I'm good, sir. Something I can do for ya?" Otis requested of him.

"Actually, I need to go somewhere in the morning. I need to meet someone at the marina, and then we will go from there, okay?" Creed informed him.

"You taking a boat ride, sir?" the giant asked.

"Maybe, I'm not sure yet," Creed answered. "If I do, it will be to an island called Twisted Oaks."

Otis's eyes grew big, and then he nodded his head and said, "I'll make the arrangements, sir."

"Okay, thank you," Creed replied. "And have a good night."

"You do the same, sir," said the brawny, solid man. And then Creed shut the door for the last time that night. He needed sleep, and he was going to give it his best shot. He turned out the light and crawled into the oversized, extra soft bed. What he really needed was a dreamless sleep, but that didn't mean he'd get it. "No dreams" was the last thing on his mind before slipping off into his slumber.

Into the Light

Creed woke early that morning. He did manage some sleep but not without the dreams. It was true that what we fear in the night comes to haunt us in the day anyway. Most of them he didn't understand, and the others made little sense, if any at all. He had learned to deal with it over the years but never could make sense of the vivid dreams that seemed so real. So real, that as a young boy, they would frighten him into wetting his bed and scare him from sleeping for the rest of the night. Often he would go climb into his mother's bed so he would feel safer. The boogeyman wouldn't dare mess with him while he was under Mother's wing, and the monsters couldn't get to him when he sought safe haven in Mom's bed. Those days were long gone and had been for decades. He was a big boy now and had to put on his big boy pants like the other big kids. Now when he has the dreams, he wakes and usually doesn't go back to sleep. Just such a dream occurred this night as well. He thought about having a couple more of the small blue pills to aid him back to sleep, but he knew this late in the game he was up. There would be no more sleeping for him on this night.

Besides, it was going on five o'clock, and he still wanted to get breakfast before leaving for the marina by seven o'clock.

He got up, turned the light on, and rubbed the crusty sleep from his eyes. To his surprise, he was famished. It was as though he hadn't eaten in days. Creed figured he should go ahead and order breakfast from room service before he even went to the bathroom. His hunger knotted his stomach, so he opted for two breakfast platters, a pot of coffee, and a carafe of apple juice. After he hung up with the kitchen, he wondered what had gotten into him—that huge burger the night before and now ordering half the breakfast menu. Maybe he was just hungrier than usual.

"At any rate, food will be here soon," he said as if someone else was there to hear him. He did talk to himself quite often mostly because there wasn't anyone else to talk to. Other than the guys keeping watch over him, there really was no one. Although he spent most of his time alone, he never thought of himself as lonely. Creed thought that by staying busy, he wouldn't tend to feel any shade of loneliness. But there were those times that he wished he had company, especially female company. He definitely liked the ladies; he simply hadn't found the one he wanted to spend his time with. As much as he worked, he didn't have a lot of time to give someone anyway. But things were very different these days with nowhere to go and nothing to do. Now it seemed time was all he had, and for a change, he did have somewhere to go and something to do. He felt the corners of his mouth turn up, and the slight grin was there again, announcing to him that this was a good day and that he wasn't going to feel as bad today as he did yesterday. And he believed that today has to be better than yesterday.

Creed went to the door and let Otis know his morning meal would be there shortly. Then he did his morning routine of a quick wake-up shower and a shave he was overdue for. Just as he was rinsing the last of his freshly manscaped face, his breakfast arrived. While still in his towel, he wolfed down the food and then a little blue pill. He was a bit nervous for reasons unknown to him then. He brushed his teeth one more time and dressed. Jeans and a polo tucked in nice should do just fine, he thought. And then he packed a small leather overnight bag. He checked the bag twice to make sure he hadn't forgotten anything. It's not like he could come right back to get whatever it was he'd neglected to pack. Then he thought he'd make sure his car was ready. Otis reassured him that it was, and Creed did the once-over to make sure he wasn't leaving anything. Nope, he had everything he needed packed in his bag, including his weapon. He didn't go anywhere without his trusty friend, Smith & Wesson.

"Okay then, ready to go?" Creed asked him.

"Yes, sir, whenever you are," the beastly man replied.

Creed gave him a smile and said, "Well, let's go then." The hulky man escorted Creed to an awaiting SUV, in which he got in after Creed, and sat beside him for the almost hour-long drive to the marina. Although Otis had the gift of gab, the ride was quiet because Otis once told him that engaging in conversation was a distraction for him while doing his duty. Therefore, Creed never spoke much while they were in transit. He used such time to enjoy the scenery since a large portion of his time here lately was spent thinking about how his life had been flipped upside down. It was nice to just take in the sights and let someone else do the driving, and he could enjoy the ride. A long section of the route was a connecting road that joined many smaller islands, so there had been an ever-changing of views depending on which island they happened to be on at the time. Creed was still a little nervous though. Recently, that had become a familiar feeling for him. Hence, the little football-shaped blue pills he was sure to pack, for the edge.

As they arrived at the marina and Creed saw all the boats, he was happy he'd be getting away for the day and the night. He hadn't been able to get away from any of it since his trouble began not long ago, but today he was. There must have been nearly two hundred boats docked at the huge facility, but the marina had a well-placed map and legend of where everything could be easily located within the compound. The driver quickly found number sixteen and drove his two passengers to the particular dock they needed to meet their expecting party. The driver eased to a stop, and Otis stepped out, not waiting for his door to be opened by his chauffer. They looked around to make sure it was all clear and then motioned to Creed that he could safely exit the vehicle. He did, and the two men made their way along the dock. Just as they approached sixteen, a man climbed out from the cabin below—not at all the professional that Creed had spoken with the night before. He thought the age may be about right, but this guy must've been a boat hand by his appearance. He was an older man of his early forties, but he was dressed in a purple leopard print tank top and orange cargo shorts with a pair of purple deck shoes. To his surprise, when the man spoke, it was the same voice as the one on the phone.

You gotta be kiddin' me, Creed thought.

"Whoa," the guy blurted when his eyes met Creed's. "You can only be the man I'm waiting for. Creed, I'm Ray Nussbaum, and we are all on a first-name basis," he said as he extended his hand to shake.

Creed took his hand to shake and then attempted to make introductions for the guard at his side.

"That won't be necessary," Ray announced and then turned to the big man. "How ya been, Otis?"

"I'm good, sir, I'm good," Otis answered.

"That's good. Your brother doing okay?" Ray inquired.

"Yes, sir. He's good, and my mama finally recovered from her knee surgery," he replied.

"Yeah, that's what I heard. I hope she liked the flowers and fruit basket we sent. Caroline said she did," Ray said.

"Oh, yeah, she sent Ms. Caroline a real nice card. She's always been so good to my mama and us." Otis implored.

"She tries." And the two men smiled in admiration for her.

Creed couldn't help himself but ask, "How do you two know each other?"

Neither man acknowledged his question, and they just continued their chatter about how life had been. Then Ray tipped his head back in one single nod to "Otis the Amazon" and asked, "It's uncanny, isn't it? The resemblance, I mean. It's downright striking, I think."

Otis bit the inside of his lip and shook his head. He glanced over to Creed and did a once-over of his face before he answered.

"To say the least, it's uncanny. Striking is good too."

Creed's frustration was on the rise, and he was at a loss trying to piece together what was really going on. And what resemblance did Ray mean? And how would Otis know of a resemblance and to whom?

"I want to know what's going on here?" Creed demanded.

Then another thought came to mind. "And, Otis, I asked your brother if he'd ever heard of Caroline Louder. He said that he hadn't. Why would he lie to me?"

"Oh, he didn't lie to you, sir. He told you, he couldn't say that he had and still can't. It's a private agreement we have. None of us know nothin' about nothin', and it works best for everybody that way." The behemoth explained.

"How does your mother know her? And what resemblance are you referring to?" Creed insisted, his frustration being heard in his tone.

"Otis's mother worked for the family for years. She worked in the house and remained close with them after her employment was finished. Now her twin boys work for Caroline. They're part of her personal security entourage for when she has to travel, which isn't much. Therefore, she's provided them for you during this time." Ray informed him.

"That explains why my checks keep coming back. I thought maybe I had an anonymous donor helping pay the bill," Creed said. Secretly, he was hoping that was the case. That there were actually people left out there who supported him and saw his side to the whole tragedy. That he was doing his job, nothing more, nothing less, serving as he'd always wanted to.

"So your donor isn't anonymous anymore." Ray concluded for him.

Lost, Creed could only stare as all of his thoughts ran together. He didn't know which of his next hundred questions he needed to ask first. There was so much playing out before him; it was difficult trying to absorb it all.

Then Ray tried to deflect the obvious. "Caroline was just trying to keep you safe. She knew they could do the job, and they did. You're here."

After a moment, Creed finally spoke. "Why the secrecy? I really don't understand."

Ray sighed and gently replied, "It's no secret, she wanted to keep an eye on you and to make sure you were okay. But she seems to think you're not okay, so now I am here because clearly I wouldn't be here if you were. Caroline is always right about such things. So tell me, are you ready to go?"

Creed could only gaze; he had no words. Inside, his still revelry was mass confusion, not sure that going on a boat ride with the weirdo was a good idea. Yet at the same time, he had developed a deep desire to find out about his family. He really wanted to go but had a last-minute hesitation due to the last-minute information—bewilderment at its best. The suspense driving him to madness and the notion that he would never forgive himself if he didn't get on that boat right then determined his next move. Without the words that he couldn't seem to find anyway, he stepped from the dock and aboard what turned out to be Ray's personal vessel.

Ray asked Otis if he would mind untying the boat's ropes, and Otis was always happy to oblige. Creed, coming back to reality, noticed Otis wasn't joining them.

"Otis, aren't you supposed to be coming too?" Creed asked in a hurry as to not leave the man behind.

"No, sir, you won't be needing me if you're going with him," Otis replied. "You most certainly won't be needing me, but I promise ya I'll be waitin' right here when you come back tomorrow."

Ray reached down to his side and picked up his captain's hat. He positioned it perfectly on his head and then turned to Creed, and with a smile, he announced, "You can call me Captain." Ray laughed, and Creed did find it a little funny. In the getup he had on, with the white captain's hat and black brim, it was kind of funny. It did lighten Creed's mood some, and he could use all of that he could get. He hadn't had much in the laughter department lately. And although Ray wasn't what Creed expected, he wasn't so bad either. He was different, but he had personality and a good sense of humor Creed would learn.

As they pulled away from the dock and the huge marina behind them became smaller, Creed grew increasingly curious about their destination. He spoke up to be heard over the sounds of being on the water.

"I tried to see pictures or maybe a map of the island you mentioned online, but I couldn't find anything nor could I find out much about Caroline. Can you tell me why?" Creed inquired, hoping that direct questions would get direct answers. And as if the captain had read his mind, he began explaining to Creed the answers before he could ask.

"Yes, I can," Ray said in his own charming yet easy to understand way. "You see, Caroline is a tad eccentric. Okay, she's a lot eccentric and a recluse, except for the extreme situation that calls for her to mingle with the rest of the world. And believe me, I do mean extreme. She hasn't left the island for years. Heaven and earth will have to move before that happens."

Creed interrupted with, "Why?" his curiosity running rampant. The more Ray said, the more he wanted to know.

"Its just who she is now, that's all. She doesn't like people much, except for us that live there with her. She's a very private person," Ray told him.

"You live there too?" Creed asked, surprised by this.

Ray snickered and said, "Yep, as a matter of fact, I do. I know this is all comin' to you really fast, but try to keep up. There's a lot to know, and it'll require your undivided attention. Got it?"

Creed wasn't sure what he meant, but he agreed anyway. Then he continued his line of questioning.

"So what can you tell me? Since I couldn't find much from the information highway other than her foundation."

"The foundation is a way to give back. Although she doesn't live like most people in society, it doesn't mean you shouldn't help your neighbor. And as far as her other personal info, you probably won't find that either. She does her best to stay off the radar. The island, well, the island just so happens to be one of America's best kept secrets. It's been in Caroline's family since 1674."

Creed couldn't believe what he was hearing and blurted out, "Are you serious? 1674?"

Again Ray had a little chuckle. "Yep, I know. Crazy, right? Anyway, yeah, since before the good ole USA was even established. It's always been a working plantation of some sort. Now it's citrus, orange groves."

Then Creed thought about the stationery in which his message was sent—the orange blossom overlay. That made sense to him now. The island where she lived grew oranges as well.

Ray went on tell him about it. Twisted Oaks was nearly twenty-two square miles of which over eleven thousand acres of that was grove. Creed was astonished by the sheer size of what was being explained to him. He hung on to every word that Captain Strange said as he told him that the busiest time would be at harvest, but harvest wasn't exactly what Creed would need to concern himself with yet. She wanted a different job for him, and that offer would be discussed with her. However, he would be happy to fill in any other blanks that Creed needed filled.

Actually, there were a lot of blanks, and so he began.

"I should've been able to find at least one map. Something."

Ray replied, "That's what I meant. Best-kept secret, I tell ya. You couldn't find it because you weren't supposed to. It's so hush-hush that it only exists if you can stand on it. Oh, and it exists in that blue book that is required to be read for every new president who takes office. They get to know about it because since it is American soil, we are afforded the protection of the military if necessary, although we pay a steep levy for it. We don't really pay taxes in the traditional sense per se, but we pay, all right."

"How is that?" Creed asked. He didn't understand how that could be possible.

Ray explained further. "French claimed the island shortly before it became family land. In 1674, it was given to the Monraux family, who were French aristocrats, as a grant if they could make it productive within a decade. In five years, they cleared a big section of what is the grove now and grew sea cotton. Anyway, they could only keep the land as long as it was held by the family, and when we became the United States, it remained that way—the land, thereby, being granted as privately owned."

He continued listening to the history lesson being delivered by Captain Professor and just couldn't believe his ears. Of all the thoughts bouncing around this brain, he kept coming back to one in particular. Why hadn't his mother wanted to be a part of the family or have anything to do with the island? And what would it have been like if he had a chance to know them or he had visited such a place growing up? Why wouldn't his mother want that experience for him? He suddenly realized he hadn't known her at all. Why had she chosen the path they both struggled so hard on when she didn't have to? If she had family, why didn't she reach out to them for help? Creed didn't know any of the answers, only that he would be seeking some of them today. And Ray was right—it was a lot to take in. But now was as good a time as any to learn those answers.

"So where is the island? How far is it?" Creed asked.

"It's twenty-nine miles off the coast. It's past the Naval Station Mayport. We'll be there shortly. It's pretty today, huh?" Ray said.

"Yes, yes, it is." He agreed and then asked, "So how do you know Caroline?"

"Ah, we met in college. We've worked together and been with each other ever since. She's the best friend I've ever had, more like a sister. A kindred spirit, if you will," Ray said, and a smile appeared as he thought about those fond memories of good times gone by.

"Really?" Creed was surprised that the captain actually attended college. He certainly didn't seem the type by all outward appearances. Then he asked, "Where did you two go to college?"

Creed nearly choked at his answer. "Same alma mater as you, we studied at UF too. One of Caroline's happiest moments was when she discovered you had chosen the University of Florida to go to school and your chosen major was Criminology. She was so proud." The statement left Creed speechless; he hadn't known she was keeping tabs on him like that. His own mother didn't care if he'd gone to college, and she didn't bother to come to his graduation ceremony either. He sent her an invitation, and she sent him a congratulatory card, that was it.

"Wow," was all he could muster. He wasn't sure what was more surprising—the fact that Ray went to the same school or that someone in the family had known everything he was doing. They were actually proud of him.

"She majored same as you too. I was a double major myself, Finance and Law." If, at any time, Creed were going to jump out and swim back to shore, it would be now. A piece of rope and he could even hang himself. For now, he had no words. *He's a double major? You gotta be kidding.* As that crazy thought played over and over in his mind, he saw something off in the distance. It was still quite a ways out, but he could see it. It was land in the ocean, an island, maybe "the island." He couldn't tell from here what it was like though, but he was hoping it was good and not some lost speck of dirt that time had forgotten.

"I love it out here. I hope you do too. I'm pretty sure you will. It's a hard place not to like. Well, I suppose that depends on who you are too. Some people wouldn't care for island life, but it suits me perfectly."

"What's not to like about island life?" Creed asked because he didn't know what that really meant.

"Well," Ray said as he glanced over at Creed. "If you need a Walmart on every corner, this definitely isn't the place for ya."

"Yeah, I see what you mean," Creed said as he looked across the water toward it.

"Yes, sir. Indeed, that's the one. We dock on the northwest tip, so you won't get to see much of it from there, but Caroline will show you around. She's always wanted you to come out."

Creed didn't respond; he simply admired the approaching property, which was mostly woods from what he could tell. They rounded the north tip, and the house came into view—huge and grand, a spectacle of old money with good taste of today. Part of it was original with new additions of modern conveniences and separate suites for exceptional comfort and privacy. Each was with its own screened-in back patios with rocking chairs, wicker furniture, and nice plants. He found it impressive yet peaceful, a good place for someone to relax and forget the rest of the world for a while. It was like a piece of paradise, and the atmosphere put Creed's mind at ease. He felt good being here and was, so far, very happy that he decided to take this ride. And he hadn't even thought of a blue pill, which was good too. *Yes*, he thought, *this is a good place.*

He noticed a boy, about twelve, waving to them from the knoll near the house. The boy ran down to where they were to dock, and Ray instructed Creed to throw the boy the ropes. Creed did so, and when the boy looked up at him, he became startled and froze. His eyes were big, and he seemed terrified, refusing to look away. The look was so worrisome to Creed that he asked he young man, "What's the matter? You ok?" But the boy remained silent.

Then Ray intervened. "All right, li'l man, it's rude to stare."

The boy apologized, but he looked intently at Creed. As he tied the boat off, Creed had to ask Ray why the kid was staring at him like that.

"It's like he saw a ghost," Creed said.

"He hasn't seen any of her other relatives before, so he didn't know any better. It just took him by surprise, that's all." Then he turned to the boy and said, "If you get all your chores done, I'll take you for a ride later." The young man smiled, and his eyes lit with joy.

"Oh, can we? I wanna go for a ride. I like the boat." The boy's voice cracked with excitement.

"You got it, buddy. Now go finish your work and come see me when you're done. I'll be up here at the house, okay?" Ray had spoken to him as if he was the child's father, but something told Creed that Ray wasn't any child's father. Something was odd about that one, and he thought he knew what it was but still not sure. They both stepped onto the dock, and then Ray turned to give him a proper greeting.

"Welcome to Twisted Oaks. C'mon, Caroline is probably in the house somewhere. We'll go find her. She won't be far, she's expecting us."

Creed followed him up a slight hill with an occasional step or two built into the mound for the steeper spots of the small rise. He imagined this would be good for elderly people who may need the otherwise nonessential steps.

"We'll go in through the side. It's by the kitchen. She might be in there."

He didn't care what door they went through. He was happy to be here, and in a few moments, he'd get to meet kinfolk. He would've been happy to climb down the chimney to meet any of his own blood.

"You lead, I'll follow," he told Ray. They had neared the top and were a few yards from the porch when Creed looked up and saw her. At first, he saw just her silhouette through the screen of the porch, darkened inside by the brightness of the sunny day outside. As she moved slowly from beneath the awning, she glowed in the sunlight. The white light lit her from her feet up as she stepped out with her right shoulder out, almost sideways. Her eyes were up, never squinting from the blinding sunlight, and her chin tipped slightly downward.

Immediately, he froze midstep and lost his breath. The hair on the back of his neck stood up, and his heart stopped long enough to miss a beat or two. The likeness was so similar it was haunting. His own eyes looked back at him, and he imagined that she was exactly what he would look like if he were a woman in his early forties. Then he remembered what Ray said to Otis about the resemblance being so uncanny. Uncanny hell, it was downright scary and just plain creepy. Not to mention, the boy who couldn't take his hawk eye off of him. No, Ray hadn't warned him nearly enough about how close in appearance they had really been.

Caroline looked him up and down to see the man he'd grown into. Then she leaned in close, and Creed swore she was reading not only his thoughts but also his very soul. With his hair on end, she stared deep into his eyes. He thought for a moment his skin would crawl away, not wanting to be seen by her. Creed felt a little tremble and thought about his blue pills. *I could use a couple*, he thought. She cupped her hands together, one gently holding the other, and stepped back. She looked him over once more, and then she put her arms around him and hugged him tight.

"Welcome to Louder House. It's so good to see you, Creed. I'm glad you're here. Thank you for coming." He fumbled for words but had none. He only smiled nervously and followed her inside.

When Family Ties
Have One Bound

"Can I get you anything? Coffee? Did you eat? Bea makes the best biscuits known to mankind," Caroline said, hospitable as always.

Creed, still without his "big boy" words, smelled the mouthwatering air of the kitchen. Along with the smell of fresh baked biscuits, he also inhaled the coffee, bacon, and sausage. It was like a festival in his nostrils, and he couldn't remember the last time he smelled home cooking. But he had already eaten two breakfast platters, and he wasn't anywhere near hungry.

"Um, uh, coffee, please," was all he could come up with. He was still astonished by how similar their features were. They appeared closer in relation than second cousins. And the way she eyeballed him a minute ago had been such a strange experience for him. He was taken aback by it and hoped he wouldn't be rendered speechless much longer. There was so much he wanted to know, and his thoughts rushed like a great flood in his mind. Standing there, still holding his bag since he stepped off the boat, he thought about the bottle of little blue pills inside. He wanted a couple of them now more than ever before.

Caroline poured Creed a jumbo cup, added four heaping sugars, and then went heavy with the sweet cream. He watched in awe as her pacific blue deep set eyes were the very same hue and shape as his own. She too was a dark brunette, his a short cut while hers long midway down her back, except for the gray strands. He would later learn that she didn't call them gray hairs but that they were her "wisdom highlights." Caroline tried to hand him the cup, and there was that perplexed look on his face he would get sometimes when he was trying to understand something. He felt the neck hair rising, creepiness crawling back up his spine.

He asked, "How did you know I take sugar and cream?"

"Do you not?" she shot back as her brow rose.

Creed was steadfastly becoming a champion of his own dubiety, and he shook his head. "I do. Really, how would you know that?"

"Some things I know, some things I don't, and sometimes I'm not sure how. I just do. Maybe it was my 'inner eye' that made me do that. That's how my mama penned it anyway. You know, an intuition? For whatever reason, I just knew you liked that in your coffee. Maybe because I do too." She still held the cup, looking down into the hot sweet creaminess and then up again at Creed. "Well?"

Creed took the cup with his free hand and thanked her. Caroline motioned to Ray to take his bag to his room, but as he reached for it, Creed pulled away as if he were a child and Ray was trying to take his candy from him.

"Damn!" Ray said loudly. "What the hell?"

Caroline glared back at Creed. "Nobody is going to steal your things. What's the matter with you?"

Creed was embarrassed, yet he felt this to be acceptable. He usually had his guard up and wasn't eager to simply hand off the things in that bag, things that weren't anybody's business. Besides, he just met these people and didn't know them well enough to trust them on face value alone. Family or not, he didn't trust easily.

"I'm sorry I'm not used to that. I've been a little jumpy lately. Really, I-I didn't mean to offend anyone," Creed said, wanting to sip from the cup but didn't for fear that he just may choke on it.

Ray had taken his captain's hat off and hung it from the back of his seat before they departed in Ray's beloved 175-horsepower Yamaha twin engine, extra heavy on the bottom to compensate its "haul ass ability" vessel. He began fumbling through the pockets of his orange cargo shorts. From one, he pulled out a brown worn-out ball cap and put it on. As he adjusted the hat with one hand, he continued to pilfer his pockets with the other. Then he scored from a knee pocket what Creed thought to be a left-handed cigarette, and he tucked it between his ear and the rim of his ball cap.

The cop in Creed wanted to say something, but he didn't dare. Besides, he was a "former" cop now, never to return to the force—or any force for that matter. Who was he to say anything to anyone about what they do? The confused look on his face said what he was thinking anyway. Caroline had already summed Creed up in the first few seconds upon seeing him, and she could sense his disapproval. Before allowing this to go any further and someone actually getting offended, she brought it all to a halt with her firm but kind disposition. Although it wasn't typical for her to call someone out, especially in front of others, she had no issues with doing so if so warranted. She believed it was always best to clear the air from jump street.

"Creed," she began to say as he looked back at her. "You'll find there is no police department here. We are the police, we are the law. We have to govern ourselves out here, and we do that by having respect for one another. We all have to live here together. To each his own as long as it's not hurting anyone else. So welcome to my island. But you will be expected to conduct yourself accordingly."

There was dead silence for what seemed like a lifetime to Creed. He really just needed a moment to clear his thoughts. Needing an easy out for a few minutes, he came up with, "I understand, no problem. Can I use your bathroom?" He did need it, and it would give him the chance to pull it together and let it sink in that he "wasn't in Kansas anymore." Hell, he wasn't sure where he was, but he wasn't in the city, and clearly things were very different here. In a strange way, it felt nice too.

"Sure," she replied. "Ray will take you to your room, and when you're done, I'll be in my study. We can talk there, and then I'll show you around some if you like."

"Thanks, that would be great. I'd like that. I've never been to an island before. It's nice here, very pretty," he said.

"All right, but I'm out after that. I have estimation numbers to run," Ray announced. "Not to mention, I told Eddie I'd take him for a ride in the boat when he was done with his chores."

"Good, he loves it when you take him out on the boat," she said as she smiled. She was quite fond of the boy herself. Eddie was a good boy and had never been a bit of trouble.

"C'mon, I'll show you your room," Ray told Creed. "It's really nice too. You should like it."

"I'm sure I will. It'll be fine," Creed replied, and he followed Ray out of the kitchen and down a wide corridor. Its walls bore large framed mirrors, and the marble floors shined a bright glare. Small palms were positioned, perfectly and at the end were white French doors that opened to a patio there as well. Creed noticed that with each mirror they passed, Ray was admiring himself. Creed wanted to laugh but thought better about it. He already poked that bear over taking his bag; he really didn't want to poke him again. He wasn't exactly off to the best start as it was.

"This one's yours," Ray told him, and he opened the right side of the double doors. Creed walked in and was impressed with what they were calling "a room." It was more than four times the size of the suite he was staying in at the hotel. It too had a king-sized bed with great big soft pillows and a thick down comforter. The furniture all matched, made of white oak, and the couch and recliner as well as the high-back desk chair were made of fine dark leather. A few plants were placed in just the right spots, and there was a mini bar in the sitting area. Creed hadn't stayed in a room like this before, and he was happy it was so nice. He stood in the middle of the huge room and paused.

"Wow, this is great. This is a really nice place," Creed said.

"Yeah, we like it," Ray told him. "I'll wait for you in the hall, and then I'll show you to Caroline's study."

Creed was relieved he'd be getting a minute to himself; he needed to take a deep breath and clear his head. "Thanks, I won't be long," he replied, and Ray stepped out to wait for him. After he closed the door behind him, Creed set his bag down on the bed and put his cup on the nightstand. He took the couple of deep breaths he needed and then fished his bottle of meds from his bag. He felt shaky opening the bottle and swallowed two with his coffee and then went to the bathroom. A splash of cool water in his face would do him some good, he thought. He took a long hard look at himself in the bathroom's mirror and opted for a second wetting of his face, not sure if he was ready to hear her offer and learn about his heritage or not. Either way, he was here, and he did come for some answers. He knew he would have to face it, regardless that his nerves were shot.

He finished his pit stop and grabbed his cup before meeting Ray back in the hall.

"Better?" Ray asked when he came out.

"Yes, much," he replied and followed Ray through the grand house to a different wing, where, as Ray had informed him, the left side was his and the right side Caroline's. They were the only two that shared that wing and did so for reasons of convenience. It was both business and personal since they were best friends, and they could be closer if they stayed on the same wing together but had separate offices and bedrooms. He said it worked rather well for them because they still had nights like they did in college, and occasionally they would sit up half the night talking. Along the way to her study, Ray again admired himself in each passing mirror as he talked. Creed couldn't help but grin at the guy's vanity. They stopped at an open door, and Ray stuck his head in.

"She's in there, go on in. I'll catch up with ya'll later. I've got stuff to do," Ray said. Creed thought that Ray's first order of business would probably be the lefty still tucked behind his ear, but he had business of his own, and he was going to leave that one alone.

"Okay, see you later then." Creed then went through the open door into a room almost the size of his, and it was just her study. Thousands of books on dozens of shelves were on both sides of the room. Her ancient desk was made of cherry wood, and she had the same chair at her desk that he had at the desk in his room. The French double doors behind her were open, and the breeze blew in nicely. He thought it was the perfect office to have if you had to work in one.

"Come on in," she told him when she noticed him standing there looking at the countless books. "Yeah, I know, I have a library in here."

"I see that," he remarked.

"So where would you like to start? I'm sure you have a lot of questions both about the job and the family. Up to you, we've got all day and all night if you like, although I'm sure you'll want to sleep at some point."

Creed hadn't really given it any thought about which he wanted to know first and wasn't sure what they should start with. After a long silence, she answered for him.

"Why don't we get business out of the way, and you can think about my offer while we catch up on the family stuff? How's that?" she asked.

Happy the decision was made for him, he agreed. It would be business first, and that was fine. He waited this long to learn about his family, a little longer wouldn't make any difference. Besides, a job offer wasn't something he thought he'd be able to get, especially so soon after the incident that caused him to be here in the first place, and he was eager to hear what her offer was, although he wasn't prepared for the offer to be as incredible as it turned out to be. She had him take a seat, and then she began.

"I'd like for you to run things around here, and I'd like to begin grooming you for my position. I'll be old one day and I can't run things forever. You know, pass the torch, so to speak. And I think it should be held by blood. It's always been that way, and it should stay that way. There is so much to know, and it isn't easy making certain decisions. Sometimes you will need to be judge, jury, and executioner and make the hard decisions. It takes a person with a strong mind, an open mind to do this."

"And you seem to think I'm the person for the job?" he asked her, wondering what would make her think that he was, kin or no kin.

"I do think that," she proclaimed. "Look, I get that you have been through the mill recently, and I can't change that, but maybe we can help each other. I can help you with safe haven, and you can help me here. Just a thought."

Creed held on to every word she said, but he couldn't believe his ears. He didn't really understand to what depths she meant, but he listened intently. Safe haven on an island twenty-nine miles out with a job sounded good.

"Go on," was all he said. He wanted to know more about this job and what it entailed. On her lips appeared the same slight grin he wore, and she continued. She explained that at any given time, there are about thirty people on the entire island, all with specific duties; however, during harvest there was about two hundred. Haitians had been brought in for generations to work here long before the days of Lincoln.

Dozens of families worked for their family, and it has always been that way. No slaves but earning a real living, they were able to support their families rather well considering how poor their nation is. They can earn in ten weeks on the island what it would take them ten years to earn in their own country. They were loyal and came back every season because of it.

She went on to say that it was of the upmost importance that order be maintained during harvest because things move fast, and there wasn't time for nonsense. So far, there had been little problem out of them, reason being that there was a permanent resident that headed things on the south end of the island. He handled all of their issues, for the most part. Haitians, apparently, have their own set of rules they play by; therefore, they generally settled things among themselves. She went on to say that Phillip, their foreman, was the only one of them who came to the house. As an unspoken rule, they weren't supposed to pass the wall to the compound here on the north end, unless there was an emergency with him, and he couldn't come himself. This end of the island was the most private and off-limits. Only those who lived within the compound were to be here. It wasn't prejudicial; it was simply another way of keeping the peace.

On those rare occasions when needed, it would be her decision that would be the final say in any matter brought to her attention, the very thing in which she wanted Creed to eventually take over. In the meantime, he could learn the ropes of the daily operations on the island. Making sure everything ran as smooth as it did was quite a task, and it would be several years for Creed to learn their system, harvest being the most important. Although it seemed like there was going to be a lot to grasp, so far he was finding it to be an appealing offer, but he wasn't going to jump the gun on it before he heard it in its entirety. He was waiting for the catch. When he didn't hear one throughout all she had said, he asked for himself.

"What part of it isn't good? Everything about it sounds like an awesome job to have," he said.

"Everything has a downside including this. Sometimes, decisions have to be made for the greater good and not for personal reasons. You have to do what is best for everybody, not just you, and that time will come at some point, and it won't be easy to make certain choices. You'll just have to though. We are self-contained at both ends of the island, we have to be. And let's not forget, you can't just run up to the convenient store when you're out of something either," she answered, and they both got a little laugh.

They both noticed that the sound of their laugh was similar too. Creed didn't look like his mother, so he wondered how they looked so much alike. He didn't know he favored his grandmother instead of this mother or father. He never knew her or saw a single photo, and he wasn't even sure he knew her by the right name. Ruth wouldn't tell him anything about them, and he couldn't figure why. He was trying to understand all the things Caroline was telling him, but it was coming kind of fast considering he knew very little. He was paying attention despite the little blue pills wearing the rough edges down for him.

"It pays pretty good though. You haven't asked about salary yet," Caroline said.

"I was going to get to that," he noted out loud while giving her that slight, almost mischievous grin.

Caroline gave it back and started detailing how payroll would work, first by saying that she would guarantee he would be wealthy after the coming season because he would bonus after harvest in the millions.

"I'm sorry, did you say millions?" he said, nearly choking on his own words. He knew he couldn't have possibly heard her right. He thought maybe his pills were making him hear things.

"I did," she replied, straight-faced. She thought he may react that way and understandably so. Those were huge numbers compared to the salary he was used to. It was inconceivable to him that he could make that kind of money. He sat tight-lipped, bouncing digits around in his brain, along with trying desperately to absorb the mere fact that this was family too. He wasn't understanding the extent of it.

"Millions? How is that?" he asked, a plea for clarity being heard in his voice.

She realized he'd have no idea how any of this worked and went further to explain to him that his monthly salary set at fifty thousand dollars would be just the tip of the iceberg. The real money came when the year's season was done, and that was bonus money usually in the tens of millions. However, half of his monthly salary would be turned over for investing in other endeavors, including some underground banking. He'd never heard of underground banking or bitcoins until now, and she said Ray would go over all of the financials with him at a later time. For now, they had other things to talk about, but that Creed would need to invest money to make money, even if a lot of that money grew on trees here at the island. "Keep the flow of funds going," she had said.

"I never imagined that much money could be made from oranges. I guess I just never thought about it," he expressed with a tone that announced his ignorance about the citrus business.

"When you put it all together, Creed, it's a billion-dollar-a-year business," she went on.

"Good God, a billion dollars?" he asked while he gasped for air.

"Yes, a billion, and that's where you come in. I need you here. I don't like to admit it, but I need the help, and I need it to be your help. I can't think of a better person for it other than you." She informed him.

"Why me exactly? How do you figure I'm the man you need for the job?" he asked, still quite lost.

"Creed, I've always wanted it to be you, but the truth be known, your mother never wanted us to have contact with you. I've respected her wishes for all these years, but it's a matter of need on both of our parts that I've contacted you now. The time has come for me to reach out and salvage what I can of what little is left of our family. You have your own bit of trouble too, and I can guarantee your mother is rolling over in her grave as we speak that you are here, but it's necessary. Besides, the only time I went against her wishes was when I paid for your college. The only way for me to do that and you not find out was the essay contest."

"So that was a sham? I didn't win that scholarship fairly? That sucks, I was so proud of myself for winning that," he stated.

"Well, if it's any consolation, I awarded the second runner-up the same scholarship," she told him.

"Nah, not really, but I do appreciate the fine education you gave me," he replied, being slightly hurt since it was a setup and he hadn't earned it.

"I know, I got your card and letter. I still have it. I was so proud of you wanting to go college. I just wanted to make sure you got there, and everything was paid for, so all you had to do was study. Ruth wouldn't hear of it, wanted no part of me doing anything for you. I just couldn't stand it, I did it anyway. And with her gone, you never came around. I figured you didn't know about us."

"Obviously, there's a lot I don't know." He was as puzzled as ever. "Why do you need me in particular?"

"The blood is running thin. I don't have children of my own and no blood heirs to speak of, and what is left of the family isn't capable of taking care of a hangnail, much less taking care of this place and running it like it's supposed to run. You're smart, I know you have the ability to do what needs to be done, to do the hard things. You already have," she said.

Creed had sensed what she meant and knew she was talking about when he shot that boy, but he didn't want to talk about it right then, so he let it go for the time being. He thought deflecting would be best.

"So we went to the same university, I hear."

Unaware to Creed, Caroline read him like a book already. She leaned back in her chair and said, "Ah, Creed, we don't have to talk about that day if you don't want to. It's okay, but, yes, we attended the same school. We even shared a professor. Dr. Darrin Wolfe, fine professor, he knows his criminals."

Creed was glad she didn't pursue the other issue and went along in the current conversation with relief and said, "I didn't know that. He was actually my favorite. I learned more in his classes than I did any other."

"Really?" She smiled upon hearing that. "What did you think of my dissertation on Danny Rolling? I know he uses it for teaching now."

Creed did remember the material and was surprised to learn it had been her work. "That was yours? No kidding? That was excellent work, and as I recall, you would've had to have some inside knowledge on that nutjob. Where did you get your information?"

"I'd say it's a trade secret, but it's not. The truth is some came from the facts of his case, but Ray knew him from Shreveport. They were neighbors, Ray was friends with his kids and had sleepovers and backyard get-togethers. You know, what people do in middle class neighborhoods, in the suburbs. Anyway, Ray and I, being the friends we were, when it came out that it was Danny Rolling, Ray was happy to tell me all he knew. Anything to help me get an A, which I did," she said, still proud of the grade she made.

He was fascinated by her story, and he wanted to hear more.

Then she said, "But it's not something he likes to talk about, so I'd rather you not mention it. If he talks about it, which he might, that would be okay. I'd just prefer you don't bring it up if you don't mind. He isn't exactly proud to know someone like that."

As much as he desired to grill her on the subject, he knew he'd better leave it alone. He didn't want to overstep his bounds, not yet anyway. He had a lot more still to learn, so that would have to go on the back burner for now.

"Well, in any case, nice work. It was easy to see why Professor Wolfe gave you an A, and I used it in my own studies." Caroline felt that familiar smile, and they each shared one of the same.

One Cannot Swim but Only Drown

The two of them continued talking with Caroline doing most of the talking about how things were run and some of the duties that would be expected of Creed, none of which he thought he wouldn't be able to do. And he certainly didn't have a problem with the pay. Although he would need to start soon, Caroline seemed to think he would accept her proposal. As she talked, he began to really observe the room he sat in. He was most interested in the framed photos that decorated her walls and along with the ones that sat upon the few tables she had in her so-called library. He was curious as to who they were, especially the few that had some of his same features. Caroline could see he wasn't paying the same attention to her words as he had earlier. She overlooked it knowing it was a lot for anyone. Before she made mention of it, he changed the subject on her.

"I can't understand why my mother wouldn't have wanted to be a part of this or why she never told me about it." He paused and then said, "I just don't get it." Caroline could see it all over his face—dumfounded with more questions than what he started out with and even less answers. She felt bad for him that Ruth left him hanging without giving him the knowledge of where he came from before she left this world.

It was heartbreaking for her to see his anguish, and she hoped she could give him the answers he needed. All the while, knowing the answers may hurt even worse than the not knowing.

Either way, she would tell him the truth. Good, bad, or indifferent, she didn't want to begin their relationship with anything less than truthfulness.

"Ruth hated this place," she exclaimed.

"But why? How could she have hated such a beautiful place? It's like paradise here. I don't understand," Creed said. None of what Caroline was saying made sense to him. His mother loved the beach and the ocean, and in his mind, she would have loved it here too.

"What is one person's paradise is another person's purgatory, and that's what this place was to her. She wanted nothing from or of this island. That's why she didn't tell you about its existence—or of ours, for that matter," Caroline explained.

"But why?" he asked, determined to get an answer.

"Because this place has a dark, sordid history, and she's a part of that history. I didn't want to tell you, but I really don't think you're going to understand unless I do. I won't lie to you, Creed, but there are things you're going to wish you didn't know. I suppose this will be one of those things. So here it goes, you didn't know certain members of the family for good reason. Ruth and her parents came here when she was five years old. Over the next several years, her father began touching her, and they moved back to the mainland when she was nine. She was having behavioral problems, and her mother got some help for her. It came out in therapy what that piece of trash was doing to her."

Before she could say more, Creed interrupted. "Oh my God, what happened?" He spit it out as fast as he could think it. Caroline hated telling him, but he wouldn't understand if she didn't.

She continued, "Her mother, Eleanor, lost her mind over it and decided to avenge her daughter rather than letting the courts sort it out. When he came home that evening, Eleanor had prepared him his favorite meal, a nice surf and turf of steak and shrimp. She had enough cyanide on the steak alone to kill forty people. When the poison began to take effect and he started suffering from his organs shutting down and the vomiting became too violent, he asked her to take him to the hospital. That's when she told him what was happening to him, and then she told him why. She couldn't help herself, and I myself didn't blame her for what she'd done. I may have done the same thing had I been in her shoes. Unfortunately, at his autopsy, the telltale smell of bitter almonds was a dead giveaway to the coroner that he had been poisoned. Now do you understand, Creed, just a little of what I mean by the history here? It's not all paradise."

Creed nodded his head in acknowledgment while he tried to wrap his head around what had happened to his mother, but he had no words. His heart ached for her, and he wished he had known, wished she had told him this so long ago. It would have helped him understand better why she felt the way she did and why she was the train wreck that she was. It would have explained why she had chosen the life she did rather than one that may have been better for her and for her son. It was starting to come into focus for him. But now there was so much in his head, and he needed more answers.

"So what happened to my grandmother? I never knew her, and now I guess I know why," he inquired.

"Well, the law caught up with her before my daddy did. He went looking for her, but she'd been arrested before he had the chance to get to her. By then, it was too late. He was going to bring her and Ruth back here where they would've been safe and never found. She was charged with first degree murder because she poisoned him, you know, the premeditation factor. Or she probably would have just been charged with manslaughter instead. My daddy wanted to post bail, so she could skip out and come here, but the judge wouldn't grant her any. If she had done it here, his body would never be found, and she would have never been caught. But Eleanor couldn't stop herself long enough to get him back on the island. She had a foul temper she hid pretty well until it was unleashed, and then hell's fury followed. Anyway, she died in Lowell State Prison for women in 1984 from the cancer."

"So your father and my grandmother were siblings? Is that the line to our relation?" he asked.

"Yes, my daddy, Elliot Lenoit, and your grandmother were brother and sister, twins. They were very close with that bond that twins have. That's why he went looking for her. He felt it, but he couldn't reach her. He never got over it, and I think it ultimately killed him. My daddy was a good man, and Aunt Eleanor was a good woman despite what she had done. What she did was wrong, but she did it for the right reasons," Caroline answered.

Creed sat in silence, not knowing what to say. He understood now, the who and the why, but there was some trouble with it all sinking in. All the information was like a bomb detonating inside his head. Even with the edge curbed by his meds, his brain was starting to ache. He was beginning to think he understood his mother more in death than he had in life. More than it had made his heart break to hear, it hurt his soul and put a dent in what little faith he had. He went to church as a small boy before Ruth had given up on faith altogether and was baptized in the tiny church they attended after he accepted the Lord. Now he knew they went because she had tried to heal. But in the end, there was no recourse for her. She was lost, and he wondered if she had made it to the other side, to the heaven she tried so hard to believe in.

"Creed," she said softly. "I'm sorry, are you okay?"

"Not really. Do I have a choice?" he snapped sarcastically. He realized his tone and quickly apologized. "I'm sorry, I-I—"

Caroline was sympathetic in stopping him midsentence. "Listen, I'm sorry, but don't shoot the messenger. If you want the answers, I'll give them. That doesn't mean you'll want to hear them, or even like them. But isn't that one of the reasons you accepted my invitation, to get those answers?" She was right—it was what he came for, and he did need to know why he never knew any of his relatives.

"It is. It's just a hard pill to swallow now that I'm finally finding this out. Again I'm sorry. I'll get a handle on it," he said.

"I suppose it is a lot harder to swallow than the ones you're prescribed. And it doesn't bring any of the relief that the little blue pills do," Caroline said so nonchalantly, as if his meds were a normal topic of discussion.

"What?" Creed asked, shocked and wondering how she could've known that he was taking anything at all.

"Oh, yeah, it's one of the things my "inner eye" showed me. I know about them, and I know you drink now too. It's okay by me. You probably need them right now with all you've been going through. But it won't always be that way. You won't need them forever," she said as surely as the sun would come up tomorrow. "Don't worry, I won't tell anyone."

"How could you possibly know that?" he asked, floored by her intuition's knowledge of his habits.

"It's the gift, I just know stuff. My gift is different from yours," she replied.

"My gift? I don't have a gift," he said. She had thrown him for such a loop, and he wasn't sure what she was talking about.

"Sure you do," Caroline said to him in her "I know something you don't know" tone. "The dreams, dear boy, the dreams are your gift."

"The dreams? The dreams aren't a gift. If anything, they're a punishment. They're more like nightmares. And how do you know about them? Your inner eye?" he asked.

Caroline laughed. "No, not on that one. Well, sort of. I know when you were a child your pediatrician said they were night terrors and that you would grow out of it. But you didn't, did you? You still have them all grown up. If you would recognize them for what they are, you could understand better what they meant when you had them."

"They're just dreams, they don't mean anything," Creed replied, not wanting to believe her. She seemed to know far more about him than he thought, and it was feeling uncomfortable. He didn't quite understand how her foresight was working, but working it was, and she had him pegged in everything she had said. All of it was true, and that was just as creepy as it was bothersome for him.

"Yes, they do. You just haven't learned how to figure them out yet. You will, and I can help you with that, but first you have to accept them as the gift that they are," Caroline said, hoping she was getting through to him.

Creed didn't want to talk about his dreams anymore. He rather would have had a root canal than talk about himself. He just wanted to know more about who he was and where he came from.

"Tell me about the history here. That's what I'd really like to talk about. Can we do that?" he asked, but inside he was begging to talk about anything except himself. Caroline saw through the charade, but she would let him have his way. She could tell they weren't on the same page when it came to him. And with all he had been through, she understood.

"Sure," she said and nodded her head as a definite dismissal of the subject for now. He felt a great comfort come over him in knowing she wouldn't pursue it further. "But you're not gonna get nearly three hundred and fifty years of the history of this island in one lesson. How about we take it as it comes, one lesson at a time?" That sounded good to him, and he agreed.

"Where would you like to start?" she asked.

"Well, Ray told me some of the beginning, but I'd like to know who the people are in your pictures. I couldn't help but notice the likenesses, and I know some of them have to be relatives," Creed said. That longing to know who's who was growing ever so strong. Now that he was this close to knowing where he came from, his desire to know was at its peak.

"Ah, pics of the fam. Yep, let's take a look," Caroline said as she stood up from behind her desk from the leather chair she'd been leaned back in.

Creed got up from his and joined her by a small table at the end of the huge couch. She showed him what his grandmother looked like in a picture of her with Ruth as a child. He admired it, gazing at the woman he never knew. He was astounded at just how much he looked like her. She was a beautiful woman and his mother a beautiful young girl. He thought about how very different she looked as a grown woman—Ruth already worn-out and haggard at thirty. She had been rough around the edges, to put it mildly. It came to mind how very different his mother and he had been. They were nothing alike, and Creed didn't think they ever shared the same thought. Regardless, she was his mother, and he loved her. He thought he may even have loved her more now knowing why she was the way she was. With Caroline's explanation, he, at least, knew why. Holding the picture in his hand made him miss her more than he thought he had, and seeing them together made it seem so real—that he came from real people, he belonged to a real family. He wondered for a moment if Caroline started the foundation because she didn't have a family of her own. He thought that it was sad but didn't think now was a good time to ask.

They moseyed about from one picture to another, with Caroline telling who each of them were. From the great-great-great-grands to more recent ones, he was intrigued by them all. Relative or not, they were helping bring Creed back down to earth. He imagined what they were like in life, thinking he probably would have liked them and happy to be learning so much about them and himself. Then he came upon a photo of a brown-haired man with big wide brown eyes and charming smile. He was strapping yet had a gentle look about him with none of the same characteristics that the family shared. Creed was curious as to who he was. Before he could ask, she answered.

"That's my Luke." She smiled with pride as she said it.

"Yeah, I noticed your wedding rings. So he's your husband?" Creed asked.

"Yes, was. I'm widowed," she replied solemnly.

"What happened?" The question flew out of his mouth as he realized how rude it was when he heard his words. "Oh, God, I'm sorry, Caroline. I don't know what I was thinking."

"It's okay, really, I'll tell you. He had a heart attack in his sleep, a massive one. It was caused by a torn valve, and too much blood flowed into his heart too fast. It was almost instantaneous; he never woke up. He died about five years ago. He was a good man, and I wouldn't trade the time I had with him for anything," she said, the memories she had of him expressed in her smile.

Creed suddenly felt deeply moved by her words of her late husband. Something inside him spoke what came next; they weren't his words, but they came from his tongue. "Tell me about him, your Luke." He was surprised to hear his voice. He would've never intentionally tried to bring up memories of him, not knowing the man himself. But it was too late; the words had been spoken.

Caroline's eyes welled, but she held the tears back, delighted that Creed would ask about him. She didn't see with her high-powered perception that it was something else, not Creed, that was asking. She swallowed hard, maybe even swallowed those tears she was holding back, and then took a seat on the couch. Creed too followed suit and sat with her at the other end. She smiled at him, grateful for the moment to reminisce and began the story of Luke. Then she told him how they met in college. She was in her second year and him his senior year. He didn't go to their school but was actually at their university for an off-campus revival he was giving a sermon at for one of his classes for seminary. She heard him on the microphone preaching and was inspired to go see who was delivering it. Once she did, she couldn't take her eyes off him. She said she fell in love with the words of the sermon and then with him. All in a matter of a few minutes, she knew that was the man for her. She said they made fast friends, and he had fallen for her too. So when she finished school and came back here, she gave him control of the church here.

"Luke was a preacher?" Creed asked. He didn't see that one coming. Caroline didn't seem the type to him to be married to a minister of any sort.

"Yes and no, he was ours here on the island. But he hated the business side to the church. His daddy was one, and he wanted so much to be like him.

Luke loved the Lord and the Word but not the racket. Although Luke knew the church didn't run itself on love for the brethren alone, he just hated asking for money when the coffers were already full. Caroline told him, "It never made any sense to him to ask the congregation for what the church had enough of as it was. Anyway, he accepted the ministry spot here not just to be closer to me but because there was no need to get money from the flock. Everything needed to run this island is paid for from what's called 'house money.' We set aside a huge bankroll to fund anything that may come up. And Luke found his job quite appealing once he didn't need money for the church." Then Caroline laughed and said, "And he got the girl."

Creed was glad she didn't seem to be so sad over his passing. The good memories she shared of his life rather than his death broke the tension that he had felt since the words left his mouth. She went on to tell him that the foundation was created by Luke for her. She had a soft spot for children and the homeless. The foundation had sponsored orphaned children for almost two decades, and they were in the process of building four homeless shelters that would offer a variety of services for people that were on hard times. She told him only men of Luke's kind did such things and that the foundation being set up in her name was one the greatest honors he could've ever bestowed upon her. She said that was better than him giving her the biggest diamond in the whole world. In the way she spoke of Luke, Creed could tell she truly loved him and still did. Listening to her, he hoped he too would find a love like that, if that kind was even out there for him.

There was a tapping at her door, and when Creed looked over, he saw a tall black man standing just inside the threshold and holding his straw hat in his hands.

Caroline stood up as did Creed, and she smiled at the stranger, and Creed noticed the man was staring at him.

"Phillip, come in, this is my cousin, Creed Lowe," she announced. She then turned to Creed. "This is Phillip Soret, the man I told you about earlier."

"Oh, yeah, hi, Phillip, good to meet you," Creed said as he put his hand out to greet the man. Phillip didn't take his eyes off Creed as he shook his hand. The man was as surprised as everyone else at how much they looked alike. He nodded his head and stood saying nothing for a long pause when Caroline spoke up.

"Is there something I can do for you?" she asked him.

"Um, yes, ma'am. I wanted to talk to ya about my mama and sister comin' up to see me next month, if that's all right. But if it's a bad time, I's come back later," he said with a distant accent Creed didn't recognize.

"Not at all. And I've told you many times that you don't have to ask. Just tell me they're coming. You know your family is always welcome here," she said kindly.

"Thank ya. I sho preciate cha and alls you do fo me," Phillip replied.

"Anything for you, Phillip. You do a good job." Then she looked at the wall clock and said, "Geez, where does the time go? Let's get some lunch. Phillip, if you aren't too busy to eat, why don't you join us?"

"Thank ya. That'd be real nice," he said, happy for the invite.

"Good because I'm famished, c'mon." The two men followed her out and to the kitchen where Bea had been expecting them, ready with their food.

The Heavens Parted, and She Fell from Her Cloud

The three ate their sandwiches and were not chatting much, too busy eating the perfectly stacked Dagwoods that Bea had prepared for them, all of Creed's favorites on one roll. He didn't ask how they knew this time; he just ate it. He didn't care much about how they knew; it just felt good to have company for a meal. He had eaten alone for so long he forgot what it was like to sit at a table with people, and he was damn happy for it. Better yet, he was breaking bread with family. It was like a holiday with kinfolk for him, even though he didn't know what that felt like either. He thought about what Caroline had offered him and about what he had learned about his family, especially his mother. He kept replaying it over in his head. Then Caroline said something Creed didn't understand but that Bea and Phillip clearly did. They both said something back, and the three nodded their heads in acknowledgment of whatever it was she said. Creed sat confused and chewed food as if he were not aware anyone had said anything at all. He knew

Haitians spoke Creole, and he assumed that was what it was, but he wasn't certain.

"When we're done, would you like to see some of the island?" Caroline asked him.

"I would, that would be great. I'd love to." Creed perked up in his seat as he said it. He was looking forward to checking the place out. He would not only be working here but living here as well if he decided to take the position. Besides, he wanted to see want an island was like since he had never been to one. He thought it would be exciting to explore a new place, plus, the fresh air and sunshine would do him some good. On the mainland, he couldn't do that anymore, but here he could relax a little. He could feel the tension loosening its grip on his nerves some, and that was a nice change. For some time, he had been nothing but a bucket of nerves and change he would take.

When they finished, Bea took their plates, and Phillip went back to work. Before Caroline was to tour Creed around the property, she told him to get his gun. She said she knew he had one with him because "all cops carry one," current or former. He wanted to know why he needed one here. She reminded him that he was somewhere else, and here you just never know. Then she told him about a time when she had to shoot an aggressive wild hog that came from the woods on the east side of the island. Creed hadn't thought of it that way; he wasn't used to being around wildlife and in nature where things happen and you're best off to be prepared and able to protect yourself.

After Creed went back to his magnificent room and retrieved his pistol he holstered on his side, he met Caroline behind the house where there had been a couple of pickup trucks and a jeep. They climbed in the Wrangler with its top down, and before she put it in gear, she turned to Creed.

"We got sidetracked with the family talk, and I didn't get to tell you more about the job. Anyway, you'll need to learn Creole."

"Creole? Why? Don't they speak English too? I mean, I understood Phillip just fine," Creed replied. He never thought he'd need to learn another language.

"That's true, but I promise you, the last thing you need is two hundred Haitians with a language barrier. A misunderstanding can turn into a rebellion fast, which can be avoided when you can communicate with them. It also shows them that you have respect for them and their culture when you speak to them in their native tongue."

"I didn't think about it that way, but I see your point," Creed said. He hadn't thought about how essential it would be to know their language, but he also thought Caroline was valid in her knowledge of its importance. He figured she knew what she was talking about since she spent most of her life on the island, and if learning Creole was the downside of the job, he could deal with it. If that was the price he would have to pay, that would be okay.

"It's happened before, I'm just saying," she said.

"Really?" he asked, surprised that such a thing had occurred there before.

"It surely did in 1848. The proprietor at the time, Francis Bodier, didn't speak Creole, just English and very little French because he was raised in the States and took over the plantation in 1846. He was a cruel man and was horrible to them. He had bedded one of their women because he thought it was his right to do so. The woman he took to his bed was the wife of their priest. It was a big mistake because although they were slaves at the time, they revolted. The slave quarters were just south of the main house back then, and late one night they marched up to their master's house, dragged him from his bed and out into the yard. They circled around him, and the woman he took came to the center of the circle and stood over him while he lay on the ground. As he yelled at them to return to their quarters, they ignored his commands, and they began one of their rituals—dancing around him and chanting. She spat on him and threw chicken feces on him. Her husband, the priest, recited his prayer, and though no one so much as touched him, he began to convulse, and blisters formed on his face right before their eyes. He spewed what was described as sewage from his mouth, formed sores about his body like a leper, and then screamed out in agony before death took him. From what I understand, it was quite the debacle. So the moral of the story is learn to speak to them and not mess with their women."

Creed tried to imagine it, tried to picture the whole scene in his mind, but he didn't want to believe it.

"Good God, what kind of priest does something like that?" he asked.

Caroline smiled at him and shook her head. She put the jeep in drive and headed toward a limestone road that went off into the woods.

"A voodoo priest, they're not all Catholic, ya know. You really have a lot to learn, Creed, especially when it comes to the people we depend on here. It would be in everybody's best interest if you warm up to their culture. If you decide to take the job, that is," Caroline explained. She then added, "Which I hope you do, but I'm not pushing."

"Oh, I know. It's just a lot to take in. It's very different here than back in the city," he said, doing his best to accept the island's history.

"Yes, it is." She agreed.

He was enjoying the scenic ride down that old road. There were woods on both sides and huge palmetto palms, some as high as thirty feet tall, lining the road. The smell of orange blossoms grew stronger the farther they went, and the warmth of air felt nice on his skin. The smell of salt air faded as they drove, and it wasn't long before they passed through a corrugated aluminum wall and into the massive grove of orange trees in bloom. He couldn't help but to make mention of the great wall.

"Why the metal wall?" he asked her.

"It's for the bees. It's to help keep the bees confined to the grove, so the honey remains as pure as it can possibly be," she explained.

"That must've been a hell of an undertaking to construct it that high," Creed replied.

"It was but not nearly the undertaking it was to bring power here. The military brought us electricity though underwater piping for the barracks they built at the south end during World War II in 1943. Now that was a job from what my daddy told me. He was just a little guy at the time. The island was in a transition period, and it wasn't a grove yet, so it wasn't a loss when they took over the island. We've had a treaty with the US since 1782 that allows the Navy or any other branch to take over the place during wartime efforts. My granddaddy had no choice but to honor the treaty during the war. But anyway, I had to call them for that wall," she stated.

"So they built that?" he asked.

"They did. I made a call to the Southeast Regional commander. That's who we call when we need something done fast. And I needed it erected pretty quick for the bees," she told him.

"No kidding?" he said. Creed couldn't believe they could make a call to the military and it was done. But he did think it was rather interesting that they had the ability to do such.

"No kidding. That's why we pay the big bucks. Nobody keeps secrets and things under wraps like the US military or the government for that matter," she told him. "Nobody."

"Wow," he declared. "I've never heard of anything like that, but then again Ray did tell me this place was in that blue book that only the president gets to read."

"Yep, just him and those who are on that 'need to know' basis," she said. "That's all part of the treaty too."

"Hmm, that's good to know," he stated.

Just then, they came upon another jeep parked along the shoulder of the grove's road. Caroline pulled hers over behind the other and put it in park.

"C'mon, let's go see what's going on with them," she said. Creed didn't know who she meant, but he followed her lead. They walked between the rows of the sweet-smelling orange trees down to an intersection where the tiny stream of fresh water flowed into other tiny streams. Creed assumed this was some sort of irrigation system and stepped over it as Caroline had done. They turned down another row of trees, and she stopped in her tracks. She put her arm out as if to stop him, but he already had. Then quietly she said, smiling, "Shhh, watch this. I'll bet money you've never seen anything like it, and even more money that you never will again. I think it's magic."

Indeed, it was magic. Creed's jaw dropped open and hung there. His eyes grew big and furnished him a breathtaking display of phenomenal beauty. Just a short distance away, she stood, carrying out her daily duties and going about her day as usual. But this was no ordinary day for him, for this would be the unprecedented moment in which the course of his life would change. He felt it; he was immediately smitten by her. Her long blond hair was pulled back and fell from around the side of her neck and over her shoulder. In the sunlight, it made her appear as though an aura was around her. She had soft green almond-shaped eyes that were set inimitably apart, and her perfectly bronzed skin glowed. In her hand, she held what Creed thought was a test tube of honey. She was holding it up into the sunlight as though she were checking its clarity. Her hand seemed to be a hive of bees itself covered by a cluster of the insects and clearly not stinging her at all. Although the person who was standing near her was wearing a protective hooded suit, she was not. She moved freely about as though she had been wearing one herself. She was completely exposed should the bees decide to go on the attack.

But they did not. She was graceful and seemed so comfortable around them like she was one of them. They didn't seem to mind her either, buzzing around and collecting their pollen, not being bothered by her bare-skinned presence. To Creed, this was the most beautiful sight he'd ever seen, not just her but also the act itself of having such a calm control over the thousands of bees. In all his years, he never saw anything like this. Caroline was right again—he hadn't seen anything like it. It would've been a safe bet for her if they had bet money on it. She would have won that one. Creed stayed silent with his mouth still gaping. She slowly capped the tube and slid it into a satchel, while the bees that enveloped her hand took to the air, off to do more of their own work.

As she was closing up the box hive, she became aware of the two of them being there and glanced over. Her eyes met Creed's, and he felt frozen and excited that the most beautiful woman in the world was holding eye contact with him.

She said something to the one suited, who then took her bag of honey tubes, threw their hand up in a wave, and then turned and walked away.

Caroline waved back and then said to Creed, "Pretty neat, huh?"

"It's pretty neat, all right," was Creed's reply, thinking to himself that it may have been neat in Caroline's eyes, although to him it was the most remarkable thing he had seen a person do. It was not something you see every day, especially in the city.

Then he asked, "How did she do that?" he asked, amazed by the way she had charmed the bees.

"That's her gift. The bees are her thing. She's been able to do that since she came here. The first time her mama saw her do that, I thought she was going to stroke out. She had a blue running fit, but she finally got over it," Caroline answered, never taking her eyes off of her as she studied her every move.

"Who is she?" His open flap was now a big smile.

Caroline was still watching the young woman as she walked toward them. "That is Megan McCarthy."

There was an awkward moment of silence when Caroline turned to look at him. There it was—that look, the one Caroline herself was all too familiar with. She knew it well, and there was no way that he could deny it with it written all over his face.

"Oh, brother," she exclaimed as she swayed her head back and rolled her eyes. "I didn't see that coming."

"See what coming?" he asked, steadily watching her walk up to them. She even walked nice, he thought, anticipating the introduction with the pretty blonde. Megan was getting within earshot, so Caroline nearly whispered, not wanting her to hear her.

"Oh, I know that look. It's the same way I use to look at Luke." She was right—he couldn't deny it. Something inside him told him that if he tried to, Caroline would have seen right through it and known he was lying to her. With Megan too close for him to reply to Caroline, he let it go and didn't say anything.

As she came up to them, her smile was beaming. Creed thought it was the most attractive smile he ever saw someone have. It was as lovely as she was.

"Megan, this is Creed Lowe. Creed, meet Megan McCarthy," Caroline announced to them both.

Before he could give her his hand to shake, she put her arms around him and hugged him tight.

"It's so nice to finally meet you. I'm glad you're here," Megan said in his ear as she held him close. He was compelled to return her affection. He too put his arms around her, and with his hands on her back, he gave her a warm gentle squeeze. It felt so good to hold a beautiful woman, and he didn't want to let go. He hadn't felt such tenderness in so long; it made him human again. He wasn't sure how she knew who he was, and he didn't care; he was just happy to meet the pretty young thing.

"It's nice to meet you too," he replied, although she didn't know how nice it really was to him.

They separated from their all-too friendly embrace. Then Megan and Caroline engaged in conversation about the honey and bees. Creed was spellbound with her and wasn't paying as much attention to what they were saying as he was watching Megan's lips move as she spoke. As the words rolled from her tongue, he imagined that it danced in smooth motion inside her mouth. He thought about what it would feel like for his tongue to pirouette with hers.

It was a warm, wet, sweet deliciousness like the honey her bees created.

"So I'll see you at dinner?" Megan asked him, interrupting the fantasy he was in the middle of.

"Dinner? You'll be at dinner?" Creed asked her like a junior high school boy talking to his crush, fumbling for his words and sounding like the dork that the other kids bullied him for.

"Well, yeah, I gotta eat too," she answered as she giggled.

"Okay then, I guess I'll see you then," he said happily, knowing she'd be there and he would be seeing her again very soon.

She said her good-byes and walked the direction in which he and Caroline came from, assuming the jeep they had parked behind belonged to Megan. After she was far enough away, he turned to Caroline, grinning, and asked, "Who is she again exactly?"

With deep seriousness, still looking at him—looking through him—she replied, "She's my niece."

Creed's heart sank; the beautiful woman, one he could only dream of, was kin. He thought that to be just his luck. One he could actually think about spending some real time with was part of the family. It would figure that with all the bad juju he had, a good one was out of this realm, not just his reach. *What else?* he questioned himself. He thought it to be the perfect analogy for the saying, "You can't have your cake and eat it too." If you eat your cake, it will be gobbled up, and you'll no longer have it to look at. It was simply typical.

"Oh, great, so more family," he said, trying not to sound as choked up as he felt.

"Yes and no. My sister and her husband adopted her when she was an infant," she answered as if he had asked it instead of stating it.

"You have a sister? he asked, curious to meet her and see if they looked as similar as he and Caroline did.

"Had, I had a sister. She died when Megan was six, and then Luke and I raised her. Her daddy died two years before her mama when his plane went down on a business trip." In her expression and the tone of her voice, Creed could see what she felt was the epitome of heartache. He didn't think he should press the issue or find out how her sister passed. The joyous feeling he had a moment ago had left him in her words.

"I'm sorry, Caroline, I didn't know," he said softly as his chin fell slightly.

"I know you didn't. It's all right, such is life. Her name was Carla, and her husband was Patrick McCarthy. They were good people," she said. Then she nodded and told him, "I miss them very much."

"I understand. I bet you do." He could feel for her and her sorrow, but he didn't know what else to say to her. He felt bad not having the words to comfort her.

"Anyway, she's family but not blood. Like I said, she was adopted as a baby through an adoption foundation Luke's father started before he created the one in my name," she informed him. "So, no, I suppose she's not related to you in the same way as you and I are."

These words were like music to his ears and may have been the best ones he had heard in a long while. He felt that joyous feeling coming back, and he liked it a lot—to feel sensation that stroked him from the inside. He was thinking how good it would be to get to know her better, and dinner would be a fine place to start. He was hoping that Caroline wouldn't object to him getting to know her; even if it were to be platonic, that would suit him fine. She seemed a few years or so younger than him, and it would be nice to make friends, if nothing else, within his own age group—something of which he didn't have.

"Well, c'mon, Creed, there's still a lot to see before dinner. You won't possibly be able to see the whole island today, it's too big. But I can take you around some more tomorrow if you like," she said, leaving the door open for touring out again like the good host she was.

"Sure, let's go. I've really enjoyed the tour thus far. I think this is the most beautiful place I've ever been to. I like it here," he said in a more pleasant tone than in the previous part of the conversation.

After coming back to their vehicle, they traveled farther south through the grove. This was a memory made that

Creed would never forget, riding through the blooming orange trees down that old limestone road. A small dirt cloud tail was trailing them as Caroline drove. He would remember this day for the rest of his life, and no memory he could recollect had been sweeter than ones he had made today. He hadn't thought at all about that boy standing over his fellow officer, or even of having any more of his little blue pills, and that was a change he needed. What he was thinking was of the pretty young woman and the perfect setting of scenery and how he could be a part of all of it if that was what he so desired. All he had to do was accept Caroline's offer.

They reached the two buildings that Caroline described earlier to him as the barracks. Off to the side and sitting almost behind it was what had been the mess hall for the men who served during the war so long ago. It was still used for the Haitians that were housed here during harvest. Caroline pointed out a few other outbuildings and told him what they were used for as well. To Creed, he could easily understand some of what she meant—that there wasn't room for nonsense. This was a very productive business, and production would be all they would have time for. Harvest would be short and fast, ten to twelve weeks to pick them all. She would have to run a tight ship just to keep things going smoothly.

She finished showing him the south end, and they began to head back to the main house at the north end. It was a little more than six miles from where they were, and she took the same road back as they had come. He really liked the ride, and they made a little small talk about Bea's tasty eats. Caroline told him that she was cooking fried chicken, and hers was the best that he would ever put in his mouth. He had been hungry this late in the day, and thinking about that homemade fried chicken dinner was making his stomach growl, and the anticipation of seeing Megan again was making it knot. It didn't matter, though, because deep down what he was really feeling was a little bit of inner peace, and that felt best of all. He thought it was this place, this island and the company that was helping ease the last two months away. Something was working for him, and he could feel it inside. Whatever it was felt really good.

An Acre in Heaven Needs to Be Plowed

Creed could smell dinner as they arrived at the house, and his mouth began to water. He was hungry for more than the good food but for Megan's presence and company again. It had been quite the day to behold, and he was interested in knowing more about his family history as well as her. Caroline told him he had a few minutes before dinner to wash up, which he did. Taking full advantage of his time, he managed to freshen up in his sink, change his shirt, and add a very small touch of soft, clean cologne. Thinking it wasn't the best idea to sit at the table during dinner with his gun, he put it away and went back to the formal dining room to eat. Other meals were usually in the huge kitchen, but dinner would almost always be in the formal.

Creed thought it was Thanksgiving by the spread Bea laid across the outstanding oak table. Of the ten chairs, Creed took the seat next to Caroline as she had asked. Always a gentleman, Creed pulled out the chair for Caroline at the head of the table before he sat himself. Ray sat next to her on the other side, two seats down with an empty one between them. A plate was there as though someone was expected but hadn't yet arrived. Another woman came in and was seating herself next to Creed when he hopped from his chair to pull it out and push it back in for her. He had not yet met her, and Caroline introduced her as Gene Roberts. He shook her hand, and when he asked her "How are you today?" she raised one eyebrow and then looked past him to Caroline.

She didn't answer; she just sat at her plate, looking at Caroline. He thought for a moment that it was rude not to reply, but then Caroline spoke for the silent woman after apologizing to her.

"I'm sorry, Gene," she said and then looked at Creed to explain. "Creed, she does most of the housework and is a vital part of how we operate, but she doesn't speak, she's mute. I do apologize that I didn't inform you earlier. I think I was caught up in the excitement of you being here."

Just then, Megan came into the room. Ray stood from his seat, and Creed followed his lead by standing too. Creed was happy she finally made it to dinner, and the smile on his face said so.

"I'm sorry I'm late." Megan addressed them. "I wanted to check a few hives I've been keeping a close eye on."

"Is there a problem with them?" Caroline asked, hoping it wouldn't be something major.

"No problem, I'm just watching because they are producing more queens than usual again," Megan told her as she locked eyes with Creed and held them until Ray finished pushing her chair in for her. It made Creed feel good that she looked at him in that way. He hoped he wasn't misreading her and that the vibes he was picking up from her were genuine. He liked the way she seemed a little flirtatious toward him. It was nice for a beautiful woman to find him attractive, especially with the reputation he had recently acquired. He would happily return the playful flirting, but he didn't want to be too bold about it around Caroline. She was already aware that he had some interest in her as it was. He found there to be no need to make it any more evident. Besides, he still hadn't decided if it was taboo, considering she was his third cousin. Although it was through adoption and not blood, he still wasn't certain. He was, however, certain he really wanted to know all there was to know about her.

As they ate, they continued talking about the happenings of the grove, and periodically Ray would throw some numbers into play, most of which Creed didn't understand, but he tried to follow anyway. He was having a bit of trouble staying focused because his mind would wander with thoughts of her. He thought of how her hair smelled and how silky soft it was against his neck when she hugged him. Her shoulders smelled nice too, and he thought about how her skin would have felt on his lips had he kissed them since they were exposed with the blouse she was wearing. Now she was in different clothes, but they were still showing in the shirt she changed into for dinner. The endless chatter went on and on, and so did his imagination of different places he wanted to touch her. Even if it turned out to be wrong, his mind would still have its curiosities.

Dinner was wrapping up, and Creed was trying to figure out a rouse to talk with her some more, some one-on-one conversation. But then Caroline interjected herself into his thoughts and interrupted his attempt at a plot. She wanted him to join her on the back patio of her suite so they could talk some more. She was most interested in how he was getting along so far with having so much information being thrown at him in one day. She knew it was a lot, but she needed to make sure he was able to handle all of it. Things did come fast here sometimes, and it would be essential for him to move just as fast when necessary. Foolishness was allowed for off time but not when decisions had to be made immediately and, at times, aggressively.

Caroline offered Creed a stiff drink that he was more than willing to take, while she sipped hot tea that she said soothed the day away. He thought the same about his leaded one, and after the long day, it was welcomed. He didn't want any of his pills at the moment, but the drink hit the spot for that edge that would sneak up on him. They talked for a while about duties and more of the island's history, all of which Creed enjoyed hearing about. The hour began to grow late for Caroline, and she bid him good night. Then she hugged him one last time for the day. She poured him another drink, which he took to his own suite when he left hers.

When he entered his own suite, he felt different. He may have been in a new place for the first time, but he was comfortable. Like he belonged there and that he already spent time there, almost the comfort of home, a comfort he hadn't felt since before he had to move away from his own house, before the death threats and the fallout that followed. He changed into his sleep shorts and readied himself for bed. He chose to have a couple of his little blue buddies, hoping it would help with the sleep part, in conjunction with the few hard ones he shared while on Caroline's back porch. He turned off his light and flopped into the luxurious, fit-for-a-king bed. He imagined it to be the equivalent of relaxing on a cloud. He could feel the day begin to roll away, and he knew there was something special with him being here, some reasoning. Reasons of the unknown to him, but he was smart enough to know those reasons were of supernatural proportions, the kind that comes as a grand blessing to some and pure dumb luck to others depending on what they believe. In all reality, to him, it didn't matter; he was just happy to be there for the time being.

He slipped off into a heavy slumber that didn't exist for him anymore. For a change, he was getting real deep sleep, something he desperately needed. He had a good four hours before the dreams commenced a strange mix that ran in his subconscious like a movie reel, its film continuously spinning off random images in what seemed to be senseless succession. On occasion, the images would scare him awake, recalling one buried memory or another of something he thought he had forgotten, a file eighty-six that never made it to the shredder. He knew the problem lay in the brain, and once the brain sees the image, it can't unsee it. It becomes stored in its database, and when you think it's gone, it comes sneaking in through the back door when the conscious isn't looking, like a regular breaking and entering, coming in uninvited and taking what it wants, and most importantly, robbing the rest of the brain and body of its required sleep.

Another of the countless dreams that made very little, if any, sense at all came to him again, one he had not had before. This time he dreamt of an elderly black man that had a deep, prominent scar that healed into hard white flesh on the left side of his face with a large pit close to the middle of his cheek. He was a man so old that his once brown eyes had turned to a cloudy cataract blue haze. Creed hadn't understood what the man had said to him. He spoke in Creole, Creed assumed, so he wasn't absolute in the proper pronunciation or spelling, but he wrote down what it sounded like to be sure that if he could find out the translation, he would, at least, know what the old guy was saying. He found it ironic that he considered taking the position, and on his first night here, he was already dreaming of the people here and dreaming in another language to boot. Normally, that would be a coincidence; however, cops don't believe in coincidence, just logic.

Now awake from the odd dream, he could only lay there and stare at the ceiling. It was almost four in the morning, and he knew sleep was done for the night; he was up. As it was still too early to roam about the house, he went out onto the porch of his spacious room for some fresh air. With no moon, it was pitch black—a darkness he hadn't experienced before. In the city when it's dark, there is still a lot of light from the flood of streetlights, car headlights, and lights burning bright in the residences that lined the streets of neighborhoods, so even when there isn't a moonlit night, there is always plenty of other light. But not here, where the dark was of a kind he wasn't familiar with. It was an almost creepy dark, the kind you hope you don't see glowing eyes looking at you. Creed thought he would walk down by the water and take in the ocean air.

It was a very different atmosphere for him, and he welcomed the change of scenery. It was peaceful with only natural sounds of the environment as opposed to the manmade ones he was used to. The ocean was calm, and for the moment, he was too. The eeriness was gone, and he was left to his dark splendor. The stars were out in the billions without the reflection of the city's lights and the stars dotted the night sky, forever being seen differently. This too would be a perpetual memory, as the ones he made the day before. No, Creed would never forget this or the calm within himself he felt right then. He noticed he was near the wooden swing he saw as they docked upon arriving here. Just a few feet away, he thought he would sit for a while and enjoy this should he decide against staying. Although he didn't think he would, he really liked it here, and even at the cost of an adjustment, he thought so far, he'd like to be here and give it a shot.

While he sat in the still night, the only movement, the ocean's ebb, he was unaware he was being watched. Caroline herself, having a sleepless night, watched as he walked to the land's edge and then to the swing that Luke made for her, where he sat alone in his own thoughts. She wondered what he was thinking, and she was hopeful he'd accept her offer. Her intuition told her it was a dream to blame for his predawn visit to that special spot. Her inner eye also told her not to pry. Now that he was here for a short stay, she didn't want to push him away with nosiness. She sensed that she freaked the young man out, and she didn't like it; it was not her intention. She didn't want to scare him off or cause any more damage than she already had. She thought it would be in both of their best interests to leave it alone. If he wanted to talk about it, which she was sure he wouldn't, he would do so without her coaxing. After a few minutes, Caroline went back to bed and left Creed to his own doing. Besides, morning would come shortly, and she would see him then.

Not long after sunrise, Creed wandered to the kitchen following the scent of bacon and coffee that filled the hall of his wing. He could detect some eggs and biscuits as well, and he was beyond ready for the breakfast he missed out on the previous day. As he walked in, Ray and Caroline were seated sipping their joe and joking about something that Creed only caught the tail end of, so he wasn't privy enough to laugh along.

"Good morning, Creed. How about a cup of coffee? Or maybe some juice? You should eat something. It'll be awhile until lunch. Not that it matters, the kitchen is always open. So if ever you want anything, you're welcome to it. Just help yourself," she told him.

"Thank you, I am hungry," he said as he grabbed a mug. "I do appreciate it."

"Well, it's probably going to be a long one, so eat up. There's still a lot to go over if you're still interested," she said.

"Then I guess it's going to be long because I am still interested," he announced, eager for more knowledge about himself and the island.

"Mmm, hmm, I knew he would be." Ray teased, referring to the flirtatiousness that neither Creed nor Megan did a good job of being subtle with.

Creed didn't say a word; he was a terrible liar, and he knew it. Furthermore, he wouldn't have denied it because it was true, and he knew Caroline would see through it anyway, so why bother?

"Yep, you get one right sometimes," Caroline said to Ray.

"I will not be a subject of your ribbing if it's all the same to you," he declared with a sharp tongue and firm tone. Caroline and Ray looked at each other, and then they roared with laughter. Creed too laughed right along with them just because it felt good to do so. In that moment of hilarity, he felt a belonging, like this was where he was supposed to be, that he was supposed to be part of the joke. It felt right.

He finished up his bacon and biscuits while Caroline and Ray went over a numbers report that Creed hadn't paid much attention to. His mind rambled with various thoughts, generally going back to Megan. He was hoping he would get to see her before he was scheduled to leave later in the day. He would be disappointed if he didn't get his chance. He was supposed to go around four but was hoping to say good-bye to her first. He wouldn't forgive himself if he didn't, at least, do that. Caroline informed him that Ray would be going over some things with him that were Ray's department to handle, and when they were done with that, he could meet up with her across the hall. She refilled her cup and exited the kitchen. Creed washed his plate and poured another cup and then followed Ray to his office.

Ray's office had been as large as Caroline's, and he had papers stacked on his desk that were kept in place from the sea breeze by an alabaster paperweight. The room was nice, his French doors open to admit the ocean's wind and fresh air. There was a radio left on, in which Neal Boortz was chattering away about current government policy, and Ray abruptly turned the dial to a top forty station with the volume low so he could hear it but not be distracted by it. He had Creed make himself comfortable, and he began his spiel of schematics and then explained to Creed how he managed to turn money into more money and summarized that investing half his salary was a monumental outlet for expanding everyone's great fortune. He still didn't understand most of what Ray said about underground banking, but he got the gist that it too was another way they could increase their profits into even more wealth. Ray said it was like turning a coal mine into a diamond mine. He also went on to say that he was very good at what he did, and that's why he was the numbers man.

Still hard for Creed to believe the man across from him was the money man. He just didn't seem the part, the stereotype; whatever it was, he didn't fit it. But he was the go-to man for anything financial or client-related. Creed didn't much care either if he could do what he said he could. Did it matter if he could make that kind of money for him? To Creed, he could be a leprechaun for all he cared. Ray went over a lot of other things too. One by one, down a list of numbers and a few rules. He would get everything in a hardbound book with a list of codes he would need to know if he did stay.

"You know, I hate to be asking, but I'm curious if you've decided? You don't have to answer if you don't want to. I'm just being nosy because I'm like that," Ray blurted out of the blue, from business to personality flaws in an instant.

Creed couldn't help but laugh a little. He switched issues and was direct in asking what wasn't his business and then for him to say he was just that way. At least, Creed thought, Ray was honest about it.

"As a matter of fact, I think I am going to take it," Creed replied and felt some pride in his answer.

"That's awesome, Creed. I'm real happy you'll be onboard. I know Caroline will be ecstatic, and when she's happy, we're all happy. Happiness radiates, and there should be more of it, especially for her," Ray said, pleased that Creed would take it on. It wasn't going to be easy.

"Well, anyway, we should be about done here for now. Caroline should be across the hall. I'll get that hardcopy to ya and catch up with you later before you leave," Ray said as he stood. Creed rose, picked up his cup, and then headed to the open door directly across as Ray said. She was standing in front of an enormous case with an open book in her hand, which she replaced in its empty space on the shelf when Creed entered the room. He would have her upmost attention. She gestured for him to sit, and he did as his hostess asked.

"He didn't rattle your brain with too many digits, did he?" she asked, hoping his brain wasn't already burnt out for the day with info overload.

"No, not too bad," Creed said with a smile, seeing that it might drive someone nuts listening to what he spent two hours explaining to Creed.

"Good, we don't want that," she said, glad he didn't appear to be scared off yet. That was a good sign for her to get from him.

"Have you given any thought to the job offer? If you haven't made a decision, I understand, and you don't have to give me an answer right now, so I don't want you to think I'm rushing you. It is a lot to think about," she said calmly, not wanting to show just how much she wanted to know if he had decided.

"Actually, I have given it a lot of thought, and I'd like to accept your offer. I think it would be a good thing for me, and I think this is a good place for me too. I'd like to try it and see." Creed's answer was just what she needed to hear. Caroline couldn't contain her joy like she would've liked. She jumped from her chair and hugged him around his neck.

"My God, Creed, you will never know what this means to me. But I promise to do all I said I would. Thank you so much." Caroline became overwhelmed by her emotions, and a tear fell from each of her eyes.

"Geez, don't cry. You're gonna make me cry, stop it," he said softly with a gentle smile.

"Are you sure you thought about it enough?" she asked.

"I do believe so. I think I have, and I'd like to help you too. As you said, we can help each other," he replied.

"I did say that," she said, happy he had been listening.

Then she asked, "By the way, were you okay last night? I saw you out early this morning. Did you sleep all right? I didn't ask in front of Ray just in case it was something you didn't want him to know about."

"Oh, um, yeah, I slept very well, thank you. I just woke up early," he replied, intending for her to not pursue it.

"Was it a dream that woke you?" Caroline asked. "Or is that too intrusive?"

Creed was already aware that she would see through any lie he may have tried to cover with. He told the truth against his will.

"Actually, it was," he answered, not wanting to divulge any more about it.

"So why did it wake you from a good sleep? she asked, and Creed knew she wasn't going to drop it. He figured if he told her she might leave it alone.

"I'm not sure why it woke me up. It didn't really make any sense," he said.

"So tell me about it. What was it about it that didn't make sense to you?" she asked, curious as ever to hear what went on in his mind while he slept.

Creed began to tell her about the man and how he spoke to him in what sounded like the language he heard them speak the day before. Caroline thought it was strange that he dreamt of an old man he had no recollection of. She was curious about what he said, that the old man said something that Creed didn't understand. Caroline had to know more.

"What did he say? Do you remember? Please tell me you remember, Creed!" she asked hurriedly like someone's life depended on it. Creed didn't find its significance to be the issue she did. Then he thought about how he had written it down and put the small piece of paper in his pocket when he got dressed.

"As a matter of fact, I don't," he answered, and the look on her face went from an excited curiosity to quick dismay. Then he said, "But I wrote down what it sounded like," and then pulled the paper strip from his pocket. Caroline jumped from her chair and snatched it from his hand. She began to study it, sounding it out from what he had written to what its translation really was. He knew he hadn't spelled it right because he didn't know Creole, but he thought she could sum it up for him.

"Oh my!" she exclaimed. "Who said this to you? Who was he? Tell me exactly what he looked like!" She demanded.

Creed couldn't believe she was freaking out over it, and his contentious expression made her aware he didn't understand its importance.

"Uh, he...he was very old. He wore a loose white cottony shirt, and his eyes were hazed cataracts. He looked blind and, um, he had a big pitted scar on his cheek," he replied, confused.

Caroline went to a cabinet that was built into one of the grand bookcases and opened a drawer. From it, she withdrew an antique, oversized photo album bound with leather ties that were falling apart. She carried it over to the table next to where Creed was seated and set it down. Caroline carefully turned its pages, and Creed could see it was full of old black and white pictures from God knows when. She stopped at one about two-thirds of the way through and spun the album around for him to get a better look.

"Is this him? Is this the man you saw? Was he the one that said this to you?" she asked, more determined than before.

Creed couldn't believe what he saw and even more so that Caroline knew who he was talking about. The man in his dream lay out before him in a photo taken forever ago. By the age of the picture, he knew the man had to be long past dead. He stared in disbelief and then quietly replied, "Yes, that's him. Who...who is he?"

Caroline sighed in relief and gathered her thoughts before she answered. Then she said, "That's Buckley, Buckley Thomas. He was a free man." She took the photo from its album and turned it over to show Creed. The back of the picture was dated 1881 and beneath that 1803–1890 with his name at the bottom.

"Oh my God, that's crazy. I dreamed of this man. Do you know what he said? What it means?" he inquired. Now he wanted answers.

"I do know what he said. He said, 'Tout bagay va byen.' It means 'everything is gonna be all right.' He told you everything is gonna be all right. You don't know how good that is for him to tell you that. That's a very good omen, Creed. I'm so glad you wrote that down," she answered, relieved it was a good message and not something terrible. "Smart thinking on your part, that's just what we need here."

Creed wasn't sure what to make of it. He was still a little shocked that his dream included someone who's been passed for a hundred and twenty-five years, and he was trying to wrap his head around the meaning of it.

"Do you know how he got that nasty scar on his face?"

"It was a riding accident. Something spooked his horse, and it took off through the woods. Buckley bent down to the side to avoid a tree limb, only to have his face impaled by another. That's what is written in one of the journals," she explained.

"Why would I dream of something like that? I don't understand," he said, shaking his head.

"Because it's your gift. I know you don't want to hear it, Creed, but the sooner you make friends with it, the sooner you'll gain some understanding of it. See, your gift is like a garden. You plow the dirt, sow it properly, and keep it well maintained by pulling the weeds as they sprout. Then come winter, you'll get to eat the entire cold season until time to plant again the next spring. If you don't prepare the soil right or pull the weeds so your food can grow, your garden becomes overgrown and your yield weak, and you could starve during the winter. It really is a gift. You should treat it as such."

Creed again couldn't make total sense of what she meant by the analogies she used, but he understood the garden reference. He thought that was what she meant by helping him. She might help him get what the dreams meant. All this time, he thought of them to be worthless, but now he felt a desire to sort them out. Maybe that old man, Buckley, came to him for a reason. Creed's head began to ache, and he excused himself to escape to his bathroom and hit the bottle of pills. This was some weird stuff he was trying to absorb, and he thought he could do that better with the edge worn off. Caroline was going to have to wait; he needed a moment to pull himself back together.

Then She Sang Beneath That Old Oak Tree

Caroline knocked on Creed's door when he didn't return right away. She had no premonition that anything was wrong; she just thought she'd check on him. He seemed stressed, with good reason, and she prayed it wasn't all too much for him. Creed told her that he was fine after answering his door; he only needed the facilities. She knew there had been more to it, but for now, she would leave it alone. He obviously had enough on his shoulders. She wondered that if maybe she hadn't showed him Buckley's picture, he probably wouldn't be nearly as freaked out as he was. But had he stayed, he would eventually see the photo albums and some trust may be lost because she knew who the man in his dream was and never said anything. And trust she would need to keep. Then she wondered something else.

"Creed, are you sure you want to do this?" she asked.

He was more than she could know, but some of it had been unnerving. He thought a lot of the peculiar happenings around this place was simply par for the course since its people were very gifted at whatever particular gift they offered. Maybe the energy here made it so. Not to mention, the raw isolation of living on an island so far out in the sea could make a person teeter on the brink of insanity. Much like Jack Torrance did in *The Shining*, the desolation combined with a mental hack was a toxic mix into a psychosis that was brewing at a low boil anyway. Other than sporadic moments of the heebie-jeebies that crept up his spine, he was at ease here, and there was a calm about him.

"I am sure, very sure. I really think I can do this. As a matter of fact, if I had my way about it, I'd never leave," he replied.

"Really?" she asked, surprised he was that willing to start anew so fast. She supposed things may have been harder for him than she thought back on the mainland.

"Yes, really, when did you want me to start? I know you said right away." He wanted to know.

"Whenever you could be available," she said.

"Well, ya know, it's not like I'm doing anything now," he told her half-jokingly.

"This is true, I guess you're not. No invitation to the ball then? If you're that ready, I can make it so you don't have to go back, not even for your things," she explained.

"How is that? How would I get my stuff?" he asked.

"That's simple logistics, and it so happens to be one of Ray's best attributes. He can have everything you own brought here by sunrise if you want," she informed him.

"No kidding, by sunrise?" he asked, not sure how Ray could pull that off, but he would like to see him try. Not only did he have things at the hotel still, but he also had most of his belongings in a storage unit.

"Yes, indeed. Shall I arrange it?" she asked. He seemed so determined, yet she suspected he had some unspoken apprehension. She also thought about how Buckley came to him in his dream, how it had been a sign of promising connections to come. If Buckley came to him and had spoken to him, it was the same to her as if an oracle had said it and it would come to pass as so said.

Creed had a notion that coming here to stay would be the perfect out. He could live free from most of that horrible day's notoriety that followed him, and he could have some peace without the running and hiding. And employment sounded good too with the chance to really get to know his family and where he came from. He had a deep need to stay; he didn't want to leave, not even to get his possessions, almost as if he were already possessed by this island, hypnotized by its calming power over him.

"It is very much what I want. And if you and Ray can make that happen, I would greatly appreciate it," he said gratefully, appreciating the hospitality he'd received thus far.

"Consider it done then. In that case, there's no rush to get you back to land. We can take our time." She reassured him.

"That would be real nice, Caroline." His eyes began to well.

Caroline smiled in that all of it had been going so much better than she had hoped. He hadn't flatfooted it across the waves to run away, yet as she thought, he just might. She imagined him doing a Jesus in a full sprint across the ocean to distance himself from the things she would tell him, but he did no such thing. He was all right with it so far.

"Okay, well, I'll tell you what, go ahead and unpack your overnight bag, and I'll be in Ray's office when you're done. I need to tell him to take care of it," she said and then paused. Then she continued, "I'm happy you decided to stay so soon. I'm really glad you're here."

"Me too," was all he said as he swallowed the tears he held back.

She smiled, turned, and walked a few steps and then stopped midstride, knowing he was still standing just outside his doorway. With her back to him, she turned her head for just her profile to show and said to Creed, "I know Megan will be delighted to hear you've taken the position and that you'll be staying. I may be a lot of things, but blind isn't one of them."

Creed again was left speechless for fear of not finding the right words on the subject of Megan. The last thing he wanted to say was the wrong thing about the young woman his heart beat faster for. Then she said the words to the question's answer that he was too afraid to ask.

"I don't believe it's the taboo you may be thinking it is. She's family by love, not by blood, and third cousins that aren't biological. I don't see it as wrong. If she was, then, yes, I think it would be, but she's not. I see how you look at each other, and furthermore, who am I to judge what you do or who you do it with or how you feel. Tell me who?" Her words caught him off guard, and he stood in silence. As he said nothing, she proceeded in her steps and walked away. Creed still couldn't say how she read him so well, but she did.

Creed did as she said and put away the few things he stowed along for what was supposed to be a short visit. He pondered what Caroline said about Megan, almost as if she were giving her blessing of approval, the go-ahead, so to speak. He made a mental list of the pros and the cons, the good and the bad of what the outcome could be for getting involved with her, if she was as interested in him as she seemed to be.

Then again, Megan could just have an amorous personality, and he was taking it completely out of context. But there were Caroline's words, and Creed was well aware that she saw things, knew things without anyone telling her. Could this be her foresight, her "inner eye" seeing what he could not?

Creed made his way through the grand corridors of the manor's wings to Ray's office. The door was open, and the radio was on, barely audible. Creed announced himself, but Ray had his back to him, sitting in his chair behind his desk, and didn't hear Creed come in. Ray was looking out the French double doors that was the back wall to his desk and a nice view for anyone sitting across from him. When Ray didn't turn to him, he stepped around the desk and noticed Ray was staring off into the distance.

"Hey, you okay? Ray?" he asked as he reached out and touched his shoulder.

Ray glanced up at Creed and then back to the outside. Creed followed his line of sight to see Caroline standing under a huge oak tree a little ways from the house and holding one hand in the other, like when they first met, except this time she was slowly pacing about and talking to herself. Creed suddenly felt that creepiness crawling up his spine again, raising the hair on the back of his neck. The sensation was becoming a regular thing, and that could pose a problem for him soon if he didn't learn to accept it. But he also felt that if the people here accepted him in spite of what he had done, the least he could do is try to accept them. Everyone has baggage, even them and especially him.

"What is she doing? Why is she talking to herself?" he asked, concerned that Caroline may have been losing her mind.

"She's not," Ray answered casually, like this was normal.

"Okay, she's not, I'm looking right at her. I can see with my own eyes that she is. If she's not talking to herself, then who is she talking to?" Creed implored, needing some form of explanation.

"It does appear that way, and I'll gander to say her mama. If I were a gambling man, I'd have to put my money on that guess. That would be my bet. Yep, odds say it would be her. That and I'm privy to the fact that that's who she usually meets under that tree. Always bet on a sure thing," Ray said.

"Her mama? So she talks to ghosts?" Creed asked as the chill bumps popped out on his skin. To him, that was just downright hokey.

"Yep, something like that anyway," Ray answered. The two men watched her for a long moment before Ray spoke again.

"I told her a long time ago that she lived with too many ghosts. Then she said I was wrong, that too many ghosts live with her. It's just who she is. Give it some time, you'll come to understand that," he told him, knowing it wasn't much of a consolation but that it was the only way he knew to explain her odd behavior.

"Does she always talk to people we can't see?" Creed asked, wondering what other strange behavior she would display. Hopefully, he thought, this was the worst of it.

"Pretty much. Adam Duritz sang it best with the words 'If dreams are like movies, then memories are films about ghosts,'" Ray said. Creed thought about his dreams and how they played like a movie.

"Sang? Who is Adam Duritz?" Creed asked.

"He's the front man for the Counting Crows, and to say he's a lyrical savant is an understatement, at the very least."

"Oh, a music analogy. I guess that's one way to describe it, huh?" Creed replied, thinking that was one of Ray's oddities.

"One way?" Ray asked. "For me, it's the best way to explain things sometimes. There's always a song that can make it easy to understand something or someone."

"What do you mean by someone?" Creed asked.

"Well, everybody has a song that describes them best depending on who you are," Ray explained further. Creed thought he knew what Ray had meant, but to be sure, he inquired a bit deeper.

"So you mean we all have a song that seems to be written just for us?" Creed asked.

"Exactly that," Ray answered.

"So then, what would her song be?" Creed asked him, thinking it might help him if he used the music lyrics as Ray did. "What song was written about her?" He just had to hear which one it would be.

"Ah, for her, it would be 'Angels of the Silences,' same band. That's the one that the lyrics seem to be solely for her, like those guys actually knew her or something," Ray said as he shook his head in disbelief still at how well that tune suited her.

"I don't know their music," Creed stated.

"What? How do you not know their music? You been trapped in a bubble somewhere?" Ray sarcastically asked. "Really?"

"No, I just don't keep up with the music scene, that's all," Creed said sheepishly, kind of embarrassed that, although he had heard of the band, he wasn't familiar with the group's work.

"I see," Ray replied, and then he spun around in his seat to retrieve a plastic CD case from the bottom drawer of his desk. He spun back around and handed it to Creed. He looked down at it as Ray said, "It's on here. It will help you understand where she comes from a whole lot better than you guessing at it or me trying to explain it."

"Oh, well, thank you. I'll give an ear to it later on," Creed said. And just to humor himself, he asked, "So what's your song? Is it on here too?"

Ray came close to rolling out of his chair in laughter.

"Hell, no, most of their stuff is too deep for me. I'm more like Tom Petty's 'You Don't Know How It Feels.' Do you know it?" Ray asked. Then Creed wanted to laugh.

"I do. Something about 'let's get on down the road, there's somewhere I gotta go.'"

"Yep, that's the one. That's just who I am," Ray said with pride.

"I've never thought about it. I don't know which one I would be," Creed said while all sorts of titles went through his head, but none really fit.

"That's easy, I know. I'm a damn good judge of people, and you would have to be 'Einstein on the Beach,' same band as Caroline's song, and it's in the compilation I gave you if you want to give that one a listen. I'm just saying… oh, and speaking of damn good, I already took care of your things like Caroline asked. Your stuff will be here in the morning." Ray had almost forgotten to tell him with the distraction of the spectacle that Caroline's pacing and mumbling beneath that tree had caused.

"Really?" Creed sounded so surprised. "But how?" It came out sounding like doubt to Ray.

"Oh, please, give me a break. That's what I do, and I already told you that I'm very good at what I do. That was just a phone call. It's child's play," Ray answered with the upmost confidence that Creed had ever heard from a person. Creed wasn't sure whether he was that good at his job or just seriously conceited. He would see if his things were really delivered by morning. And if it was, Creed thought, he just might have to eat his crow with a smile, which he would happily do if Ray made the move happen overnight.

"Okay, I'm not doubting you. So tell me, how long does she usually do that? Talk to, well, whoever, I mean?" Creed asked.

"It depends, there's no telling. So why don't you have a seat? She'll be looking for you when she wraps that up, and she said you'd be coming in here," Ray said as he extended his arm out for Creed to sit in the same chair he had the day before.

Creed did as he said and sat, but the creeps still hadn't left him. He wasn't sure what to make of any of them, and he was doing his best "not to judge a book by its cover," like Caroline suggested yesterday. She told him that wouldn't do him any good here. The people on this island were gifted, all of them, and they were all the best at whatever their gift happened to be—Ray with the money and the ability to make things happen and Megan with the bees. Then there was Bea's incredible cooking and Caroline's knack for seeing right through people, almost like she could read their thoughts. Not to mention, the doctor who lived there and whom Creed had not yet met.

Caroline said he was the finest trauma surgeon in the country and a hell of a fine doctor. When Creed asked her why he was here instead of saving lives on a daily basis at some hospital somewhere, she told him it was because he had come to hate most people. She said what he hated most was the way he felt about the lives he saved. All life is supposed to be precious, but in his mind, some lives had become more valuable than others. Therefore, he had no business at a hospital anymore; he was on permanent sabbatical as far as the rest of the world was concerned. He wanted to save the girl who was her high school's valedictorian and who earned a scholarship for her academic achievements and who had been involved in a car crash, but he found it difficult to want to save the life of the young man with five bullets in him because he was shooting up his neighborhood, and someone finally shot back, giving him a lifetime in a wheelchair to look forward to. Then when you tell his family he'll never walk again, his mother falls out on the floor wailing and howling that he can't walk instead of being grateful her son was still alive. And God forbid he couldn't save the young man's life— that was worse. There were times families threatened to kill him because the patient was DOA and beyond saving. That would usually turn out to be his fault somehow. It got old, and now he's here, serving as their doctor and living away from the kinds of people he loathed.

After a while, Caroline made her way back into Ray's office as if nothing she was doing outside was abnormal. Ray asked her if everything was all right, and she said she wasn't sure but that so far she thought it was. Ray said nothing more about it, and they made some talk about the estimation report he had given her the day prior. Creed got the gist that they were expected to have an extremely profitable season with this year's harvest. Creed's thoughts drifted back to Megan and her beautiful smile. He was hoping to see her sometime before dinner, but if mealtime was to be the only time he saw her today, that would be okay too as long as he saw her. Although Caroline said she didn't have a problem with his interest in Megan, he really wanted to get Megan's opinion, if she even thought of him in the way he thought of her. That remained to be seen and a whole different ballgame from any interest he may have had for anyone else in his past. She wasn't like anyone he had met before, and his desire to know her better burned in his gut like a three-alarm fire he had no plans to extinguish. His fiery thoughts were interrupted, and he discovered Caroline was very good at intruding upon this imagination when he was carried away by his lecherous thoughts of her.

"What? I'm sorry, what did you say?" Creed asked.

"Weren't you listening? Where were you, daydreaming?" she asked Creed with the sarcasm of a schoolteacher when caught sleeping in class.

"Uh, yeah, I must've been. I'm sorry, what did I miss?" Creed asked, hoping it wasn't too important that she would be disappointed for his lack of attentiveness. He couldn't help himself but think of Megan; he couldn't seem to get his mind off of her.

"I was just saying that we could go around, and I could show you some of the other places on the island, so you could get familiar with where everything is," she answered.

"Ya know, it is an island, Caroline. It's not like he's going to get lost, and even if he does, he won't be too hard to find," Ray said.

"Yeah, right, remember when Eddie was lost in the woods? It took us almost all night to find him, and when we did, he was eaten up with bug bites so bad that he was sick for two days from it. I'd rather not have a repeat of that if I can help it," she replied.

"Yeah, those woods can be tricky," Ray said.

Creed thought if they went out touring again, he may run into Megan once more, and he was all for that idea. Besides, he liked it here and wanted to see some more of it anyway.

"That would be good. I'd like to see the woods you mentioned," Creed said, eager for a chance run-in with the pretty woman that was holding his thoughts hostage.

"Oh, there's a lot more to the woods than just woods. I'll show you where the other places are that you'll need to know," Caroline said. "Bea is busy taking care of some things, so I'll pack us a lunch. We won't be back for a while."

"Sounds good to me, can't wait. I'll help with you with the lunch," Creed said happily. He was overjoyed they would be going back out, and he would get to see more of this place that made him feel at peace.

Caroline smiled at his willingness to help her with something as simple as making a couple of sandwiches. She was relieved he stayed, and even better, he was happy to be so helpful.

"Sure, you can help, c'mon," she told him, and then they both said their good-byes to Ray and left him to his office, alone.

A Lighthouse
Was Buried Beneath the Sea

Creed took the CD Ray had given him to his room since he would need to get his pistol anyway. Like Caroline schooled him the day before, he shouldn't leave the main house without it. Then he helped her with the brown bag preparations of lunch, and they set off from the house. Once they were through the gate and past the excessive wall, she turned the jeep left, this time down a different road paved with the same lime rock as the one from his first sightseeing trip through the grove. This road went around the southeast side of the island and would end where the Haitians lived from what Caroline said—well, the only ones who were there this time of the year. During the off-season, there were always between eighteen and twenty Haitians that stayed on for the continuous work that was still required.

They had driven barely a mile into what seemed like woods when they came around a bend that then opened up into a clearing. There were a few outbuildings and then a nice cottage with a couple of rocking chairs under a shingled awning and flower boxes beneath the window frames in bloom. Caroline told Creed it was the home of the doctor and his wife, Maureen—called Mo for short. Mo's job here was to run the storehouse and order supplies that came in twice weekly. Everybody had a job to do of some sort, and she was who he would turn in his supply list to. Anything he needed or wanted, she could get.

"Besides, it keeps her busy and her nose out of the romance novels. That drives Doc up a wall," she said.

Creed couldn't help but laugh out loud. He could see how that could drive a man crazy, especially a man who spent a decade in medical school. The last thing a man like that needs—or any man for that matter—is a wife sitting at home, wishing her husband would love her like in the stories she read. Meanwhile, she never for a moment takes into consideration that it's all make-believe and fantasy, or how he's overworked at ninety hours a week at an overworked and understaffed hospital that's always short of beds. She doesn't think about how exhausting the sixteen-hour, sometimes as much as twenty-two-hour, surgeries he took an oath to perform are. No, she wants wine and roses every night and for him to sweep her off her feet every day. Maybe in a perfect world, but if it was, there would be no need for his skills or the hospital he worked in. That's not the world we live in, and it never will be. Then Creed had another thought—smut like that should be banned—and he laughed out loud again.

About another tenth of a mile past the cottage, the woods opened up again. There were two huge warehouses on the left and a building on the right that Creed had to ask what it was used for. Caroline explained that the two on the left were storehouses for supplies; everything was in there, and the one on the right was a medical unit for routine or emergency care. There was also a small dental facility behind it, but the dentist had to be brought in.

Caroline eased to a stop in front of the first of the two storehouses.

"C'mon, we'll go in and say hi," she said, and then she stepped from the vehicle. Creed followed her through the door where she introduced Mo and Creed. Caroline informed Mo of him taking residence and told her he was welcome to anything in supply and to order anything that may not be, if he so asked. Mo smiled at Creed and nodded her head.

"Yes, ma'am, you got it," Mo said kindly.

Caroline and Mo chatted a few more minutes as Creed eyed all of the goods stored in the big facility, and then they were on their way south again. The winding road would cut through the trees and along the coastal side. This is where he discovered the island's namesake. The enormous oak trees along the cliffs were twisted toward the west from the undying sea wind in a perpetual backward bend. All their limbs intertwined with each other like a chaotic wooded weave. Creed told Caroline he understood where the name

Twisted Oaks originated, and she explained that it was given when their ancestors first arrived, except it was in the French translation of "Tordus Oaks." Over the years, it converted to its American name. Creed also voiced his opinion of it being one of the most interesting things he ever saw. In all his life, he never saw trees bow over like that. Caroline thought so too.

Before the road turned back into the woods, they came upon a large mound of white dirt just before the curve. Caroline slowed, and Creed asked to stop. He could see that past the small hill, it was open, and he thought he could get a nice view of the ocean. She parked, and the two of them got out. Creed crossed over the mound, and the view of the water was spectacular. For as far as the eye could see, it was perfect seas. Creed was captivated by the ocean and the hold it was beginning to take on him. Although Creed knew the sea was unforgiving in its great power, it was beautiful, and it had a calming effect over him. Even with trying to adjust to all the recent changes in his life, this place made him feel a bit relaxed, and he was starting to think he was going to be all right.

"What was this place? What was here?" he asked Caroline.

"It was an old lighthouse," she replied. She had hoped he wouldn't think too much of it.

"What happened to it?" He persisted.

"It was torn down a long time ago," she answered, but she could tell he really wanted to know and that he wasn't going to relent. She thought it was just his nature—that cop part of who he was.

"Why? I mean, wouldn't that be worth saving?" he asked.

"No, it wasn't," she said.

"How do you prevent shipwrecks without it? Isn't it needed?" he asked.

"Not really. No one can get within five miles of this place without the military stopping them," she answered.

Creed could tell by her short answers that she didn't want to talk about it for some reason, but if he were going to be living here, he should know everything.

"I had the lighthouse demolished and carried out to sea the same day the acquisition papers were finalized."

"But why?" he asked again. Now he really wanted to know.

Reluctantly, she knew she had to tell him the truth. He wouldn't stop until he got it, even if a lie would've been better.

"Be careful what you ask for, Creed. You just might get it. There's a dark history here that should be buried, but you should get the truth if you ask for it. Just remember, though, the truth hurts, and what you find out, you can't unfind. You know it forever. And since you're not going to let a sleeping dog lie, well, the truth is that this is where Ruth's daddy used to bring her for his dirty deeds. I tore it down for Ruth. Not that it mattered, she still didn't come back," Caroline answered, hating the sound of her own words. "But I did it for her, one less reminder."

He stood, silent, glad for the honesty but wishing he hadn't asked. He could feel his heart breaking for the mother he no longer had. Caroline was right—he didn't like what he'd heard. At least, she told him the truth, as hurtful as it was. He was understanding more about his mother, a woman he thought he knew, but he was getting closer to her in death than he had felt in life. He felt sad for her, and he wished he could hug her again. Hearing the things she went through made him wish he could help her, but there was no helping the dead, just the living. He was so disgusted by being in the very spot his mother spent her entire life running from. He felt sick and told Caroline he was ready to go. Without hesitation, she obliged, and they left the mound.

She drove away from the coastline and followed the road through another patch of woods. Again it widened where they came upon ten more cottages, smaller than the doctor's. There were five on each side, and they looked vacant to Creed, but he didn't ask about them. His mind was still on his mother and the atrocities she had endured, his emotions mixed. He was beginning to love this place and to feel real peace about his own recent history, but he hated the island's dark past. He knew deep down that he had only scratched the surface of its moroseness. He thought that if the tip of the iceberg was this bad, the iceberg itself could possibly be worse than he imagined. He didn't want it to be, but it seemed like the only good was in its scenery. He wasn't sure if that would be enough to overcome its wretched history, but he did know this—history doesn't repeat itself; people repeat history. And with the sense the people here seemed to have, maybe there wouldn't be any repeats of the darkness of the past.

As they continued to drive, they came to a fork in which Caroline took to the right. She said this road would cut through to the third and last of the roads that ran from the north end to the south end. It was the central road that wasn't used much, but it was traveled heavily back in the "old days." As they made a left turn onto the central road, Creed mentally noted his whereabouts for future outings he'd like to take. He was always good with direction, and he didn't foresee ever getting lost as long as he stuck to the roads. They hadn't been on the road long when Caroline slowed down to a stop, and Creed saw why. To their left, he could see nearly a hundred headstones. Most were ancient and some unreadable until he got closer. They walked into the family's burial plot while Caroline told him about it. A lot of their ancestry was right here, buried six feet deep. She said she liked it here in the cemetery. He found that a strange thing for a person to like, but she did talk to ghosts, and that was even stranger.

As he walked, he came to one that caught his eye. It bore Carla McCarthy's name with her birth date and death date.

It had a remarkable slab of marble completely covering her grave and fresh flowers in its vase.

"This is your sister's, right? You said her name was Carla."

Somberly, Caroline closed her eyes, bowed her head, and nodded. It still hurt her so bad to come here, but this was where her loved ones were. And that she had been compelled to come here since early childhood. She felt connected to them by visiting the graveyard. Then she said that Megan must've brought her mother the flowers. She was going to do it today, but Megan beat her to it. Creed picked up on Caroline's desire to not discuss it and didn't push. He made that mistake already where the lighthouse had once stood and thought better to just drop it than to ruffle her feathers. She was easy to read when she didn't want to talk about a subject. Although he did wonder what happened that was so bad that she felt the need to keep quiet about her sister's untimely death. It was evident she was too young to have passed naturally. Good sense would beat out his need to know this time.

"They're pretty. Are those lilies?" he asked.

"Yes, they're peace lilies. They were Carla's favorite. We have a whole garden of them just past the other gardens. We grow them special, just for her," Caroline said.

"She must've been very special. That's a good thing of you to do for her," he said. Then he thought about how long it had been since he placed flowers on his own mother's grave. It had to be at least seven or eight months, and he felt crappy that he hadn't taken better care of her grave. After all, he was the only one who ever visited her six-foot earthen resting place. He wished he had done more.

"She was and still is. She's missed very much," Caroline said. Then she turned and headed back to the jeep. Creed didn't say anything else; he let her go and began to follow her. He looked around upon leaving and noticed Luke's grave as well. His had a marble slab with an ornate marble cross that rose up almost eye level from his marker. Scattered around his plot were little crosses that had been whittled from various types of wood. Most of them were worn from the elements, but Creed could tell at least two of them were put there recently and not yet degraded by exposure to the climate. He was curious about them but assumed now wasn't the time to ask about those either.

They continued on their journey of familiarizing Creed to the island. He enjoyed the sights and found himself relaxing as they drove. There was still a lot he didn't like about this place's terrible past, but it seemed to him that Caroline was doing all she could to erase what she could and oppress the rest. He knew there was so much more he wasn't aware of yet, but he was hoping he could take it. After all, he thought, he was a cop not long ago and had seen it all during his short career. Besides, he had so much more to learn about his roots, and so far, it had been interesting to find out. Caroline had given him more information in the day he had spent here than he had ever learned from his mother, and he was grateful for what he did know.

Caroline turned off the middle road onto one that went through the grove. He loved all the different fragrances, especially the overwhelming blossoms that covered every orange tree he could see. She told him all that the island offered in the different outdoor activities. There was a beach and a lagoon with several fishing docks and boats and jet skis he could use at his leisure. She explained there were several floating docks around the island that had nice benches from which he could just sit and enjoy the serenity of his surroundings if he liked. He was listening, but he was thinking about Megan and hoping they would have a chance run-in again before dinner.

"Ready for lunch? I'm kinda hungry myself," she mentioned.

"Sure, I am too," he said.

They stayed on the same road until finally they reached the end. It opened on the pristine white sand shore of the lagoon. It was breathtakingly beautiful and an ideal place to eat their sandwiches. The more of the island he saw, the more he believed he made the right choice. Even if there were strange happenings, it was better than running and hiding the rest of his life. He thought if he gave it his best effort, he could be happy here. All he had to do was remind himself every day that this was better than what he could have back on the mainland. He could have more than he ever dreamed of if he played his cards right on this. And he would be a fool not to; he could have it all, and he knew it.

Creed was a lot hungrier than he thought and inhaled his sandwich in five bites. As he ate, Caroline talked some more about operations and such while he admired the view of the lagoon. It's sandy shore and clear water were inviting, and he wondered how soon it would be until he could get in it. It was perfect for an afternoon swim, and a quick dip on such a hot day would be the height of anyone's day. He knew the moment would come at some point for him, maybe not today but someday soon. He thought it would be nice to take a swim with Megan or maybe skinny-dip with her, but for now, that would be his own personal fantasy that no one needed to know.

"Creed, are you listening?" she asked, and by the startled look on his face, she knew he wasn't.

"I'm sorry, I guess I got caught up in all there is to see here. I haven't seen the beach in so long. I must've gotten lost for a minute there," he answered, embarrassed. He seemed to be doing a lot of that lately, and he figured he should try to break himself of it. That wouldn't be a good habit to get into.

"It's all right, c'mon, we should be heading back. I need to check some trees that Jean said I should look at," she informed him. "He's one that stays on year-round and does most of the tree inspections. He's real good at grafting them too. He thinks some of the young trees may try to produce too early, and I need to check it out."

"Okay, you're the boss," he replied.

"That's the rumor, anyway," she said, and they both got a good laugh. They gathered there lunch bag trash and went back to the jeep. Down the road a ways, they passed another jeep and a pickup that were parked on the side of the road. Neither of which he saw the previous day, and he just assumed they belonged to workers from the south end of the island. Caroline kept going for another half mile when she pulled over, and they both took one of the paths through the grove to an area of small trees that were planted in large plastic containers that were set into the ground about a foot deep. All the saplings and blooms, Caroline carefully inspected. One by one, she would examine their blossoms and their leaves, turning them over and rubbing a leaf between her fingers every so often. Creed didn't know exactly what she was looking for, so he asked. She explained that she was checking their development.

"Well? Are the trees all right?" he asked curiously.

"That's just it, they're more than all right. They couldn't be better. Now if the fruit they bear is sweet, we may have hit the mother load. As if we hadn't already. Gold grown from the earth and all its eminence and superior reverence." This was spoken like a guru who had all of life's answers. "It's a blessed phenomenon, Creed, a miracle of something greater than us, a tipping of the hat and a pat on the back from God himself with an 'Attaboy.' You see that, don't you?"

And he did see that, along with a great deal of other things he saw as well. Some of it he most certainly didn't like. The creepiness, he called it, but it was still a good trade-off since he could live free by relocating to the remote grounds. He had given it some thought and decided, while his nerve was up with the blue pills he consumed with his lunch on top of the two he had before breakfast, now was the time to ask about that solo chat she had under the tree.

"I do see that. I see something else too. The trees are great, but how are you?" he asked with the same expression on his face as she would have on hers if she had been asking—serious yet soft and kind and full of understanding.

Caroline knew partially that in his asking were his meds. Taking the edge off had a tendency to allow that. But there was something else she saw; after all, he wasn't that hard to read.

"Perception getting better? Are you tuning into it?" she asked him with a slight grin. Maybe he was beginning to read her, and she wasn't fond of that theory. "What do you think you see?"

"I don't think I know. You were talking to yourself under that tree. I saw that with my own eyes, I'm not blind. Why do you do that?" he asked in that same sharp tone as hers when she's inquiring.

"Ah, that's what you mean. It may have appeared as such, but, no, I wasn't talking to myself, and I'm not crazy. I happened to be talking with my mother. My loved ones that are long since gone come to me in several ways, and that's my mother's way of stopping by. They tell me things, the things I need to know. Call it what you will, but I like it that I can still see them and talk to them, sometimes offering good advice or guiding my intuition with a foresight that will help me through whatever peril is to come. They don't show my everything, but I get some good insight on some of the important stuff. So, yes, I'm fine, Creed, and quite frankly, I don't expect you to understand it, not this early in our relationship. You don't know me that well yet, but it's good to know you would attempt to try."

"I meant no offense. I'm just trying to understand, that's all. And I apologize if I did offend you, it wasn't my intention," Creed said, hoping he hadn't hurt her feelings in any way.

"None taken, I'm just saying I'm not a psycho. I just see what others do not. I'm in tune with my gift, my mind, and who I am," Caroline said.

"And I have no regrets of having it."

"I've never seen a sane person do that, and you seem sane to me. I've had to Baker Act people for things like that when I was on duty. It's just odd to see someone whom I believe is sane to do that. But you really don't have to explain it to me. I think I understand," he said, and he was starting to understand slowly but surely.

"Do you?" she asked. She wondered how he could possibly be understanding any of it. But she would give him the benefit of the doubt.

"I like to think I do or, at least, I'm trying to," Creed stated with a hint of uncertainty.

Caroline smiled softly at Creed. "C'mon, let's get back to the house. It won't be long before dinner, and we should wash up. Besides, I wouldn't want you to miss out on the good eats or Megan's company." Then she laughed out loud.

"Haha, very funny," he said and gave her a familiar half grin.

She shook her head, and then the two made their way back to the side of the road where the jeep was pulled off on its shoulder. All the way, Creed thought of the pretty blonde bee charmer, patiently waiting to accompany her again. To be in Megan's presence was a feeling all its own. He could equate it to nothing less than to sit next to the queen for the entire evening. The privilege of her arm's length company for dinner and the ballet, sharing her table and her private box at the theatre. That's what it was like, a privilege, one he wasn't certain he deserved but nonetheless would still make some attempt to talk to her. He did like her and the way Megan would look at him with a look of sultry innocence, something of wanting and liking what she sees when she looks at him but not really recognizing how purely raw the look in her eyes were, unrehearsed and naturally flowing. No, Creed couldn't wait to lay his eyes on her and to hear her voice again. He was on pins and needles riding to get back, anxious that he hadn't had sight of her all day, and he would be really disappointed if she didn't make it to the meal for some unforsaken reason.

But he wouldn't be disappointed after all. The food was good as well as the company. They caught each other's eye more times than they could count through dinner. One thought played like a broken record in his head—how would he even approach her? He wasn't in the city anymore, so he couldn't take her to dinner and a movie out here. What the hell would he ask her to do? Over and over, he came up with zip, but he was still determined he was going to talk to her one way or another. Creed already loved the way she would look at him, and he would never forgive himself if he didn't try to, at least, make friends with her. He noticed during dinner that Caroline would often look at them as if she could see the interest the pair had in each other, and that was a little uncomfortable for him, but Megan was worth a few discomforts in his opinion.

As the meal came to a close, Megan mentioned she had an online open forum for one of her classes she had to attend within the following half hour. Then Caroline told Creed she needed to speak with him when everyone was finished. He didn't know what about, and right then he didn't care. He wanted the chance to talk to her privately, and it wasn't looking like he was going to get to either. He thought that was just his luck though. It was always like that for him, and he thought why should today be any different than any other day; of course, his luck would suck, once again. Caroline said she had a few things to do, but then she would be retiring early this evening. Creed concluded this would be a good opportunity to consume a large amount of the bottle of booze he stashed along for his trip. He was rather glad at that moment that he had brought it with him.

Caroline took only a few minutes of his time, and before she let him go for the night, she told him that everyone was off the following day, and then she offered him a small bit of helpful advice.

"I've watched your dilemma during dinner and—" she began to say, but Creed prematurely interrupted.

"Dilemma? What dilemma?" he blurted.

"As you are not blind, neither am I. Where do you invite her to go? No top dollar restaurants or good shows to take her to out here, I see it. But if it helps, she likes lavender and gardenias. She also likes a picnic and a relaxing day at that same beach we ate our lunch at today. If I may be so bold and suggest that you go cut her some flowers from the gardens and ask her to a picnic at the beach for the afternoon. She loves to drop out over into the lagoon from that rope swing. I don't think she's ever had a bad day there. I'm just saying, ya know, trying to give you some inside information, that's all," she informed him. Caroline almost sounded like a matchmaker, but it didn't matter to Creed. He was grateful for the tidbit; it would be useful knowledge for later. After all, Megan would be tied up with her forum tonight, and he didn't think he'd have a chance to catch up with her until the next day.

"Thanks, I'll have to remember that," Creed replied, not able to hide his slight blush. There would be no hiding his liking for the young beauty.

Caroline said her good nights, so she could do a couple of things before she turned in early. Creed was on his way back to his own room for a date with his bottle when just before he neared his door, Megan exited from a door at the end of his wing. She smiled at him when their eyes met, and he paused at his door wanting their paths to cross. This could be his chance to ask her, he thought. As she walked toward him, she laughed and said she was glad to see him. Then before he could reply, she said her class would be about an hour.

"I don't suppose you'd like to have a drink with me on the back porch when I'm done, would you? Or is that too forward?" Megan asked sweetly and softly.

Creed couldn't believe this was happening. She asked him first; he wouldn't have a chance to approach her. She did it for him.

"You're damn right I would, and, no, it's not too forward. Truth be told, I was going to ask you." Creed spit the words out so fast he almost sounded desperate.

"Okay, cool, I'll see you in about an hour then," she said with her perfect smile.

"Great, yeah, see you then," he replied. Inside, he was doing a happy dance, ecstatic he would be keeping in her company.

Megan walked toward the kitchen, and he assumed she was getting a drink or something before she started her online work. He opened his door and paused for minute. So much for the bottle date, he would get a shower and prepare himself to see her instead. A good start would be a couple of the little blues to curb the tension from his excitement. The night was on its way to being far better than Creed had anticipated, and for a change, he had something good to look forward to.

From the Ashes, Greatness Is Born

The evening with Megan had gone well, although cut short due to her giving her word to help a fellow classmate with a project. Creed wasn't disappointed because he was happy to have what time he had with her. It was the best hour and half he could remember having. She was funny and personable, very easy to talk to. He felt a comfort around her that he had never experienced with anyone else before. They shared a couple of drinks on the back porch and caught the last part of the sunset. They discovered that they shared a lot of the same interests and actually had a few things in common. Most importantly, they shared an unspoken chemistry that no one could understand, unless they too had felt such stirring within themselves at some star-crossed time in their life. As darkness fell, he knew his minutes with her were numbered; he would need to ask her soon.

"I know you'll need to go soon, but I was wondering if you would like to go to that beach at the lagoon tomorrow? I could pack us a picnic if you like. That is, if you're not doing anything," Creed asked, his voice almost cracking like it did when he asked Natalie Barton to senior prom.

He knew she would shoot him down in flames, but she didn't. She said yes just as Megan had—flirty and thrilled.

"Actually, I'd love to, Creed. I appreciate the invitation. Sounds fun. " She happily accepted. "What time would you like to go?"

He was so overjoyed he could have run out the door screaming all the way that he was the luckiest guy ever. Caroline had been right—that was what Megan liked to do, so it was a good chance she would say yes, and she did readily.

"Um, I don't know, how about nine o'clock?" he asked, surprised she answered so quickly.

"That's perfect, I'll be ready at nine then," she said. Then came what he was afraid to hear but knew was coming eventually.

"Well, I better get going. I have a few things to do besides helping my classmate. Have a good night, Creed and I'll see you in the morning."

Creed smiled and asked, "Okay, can I walk you in?" She obliged, and he walked her to her room, and then he went to his own. He took out his stash and broke its seal. He didn't bother with a glass, drinking the poison straight from its clear bottle. He propped himself up with the fat pillows against the headboard and drank some more, thinking of her. He learned a little about her in the short while they had spent out back and replayed her words over in his head. She was bright, humorous, loved animals and the beach.

She had spent most of her life here and had no plans to ever live anywhere else; this was her home. She attended the same college and majored in agriculture with a minor in horticulture. The thing with the bees became her regular line of work after she moved back here upon graduating. They both liked the same things, and even some of the same music, although she didn't really keep up with the music industry either.

He lay there with his thoughts drifting about her, swigging from this bottle. He didn't know what time he had fallen asleep, but he knew it was late when he woke to realize he hadn't changed his clothes and that he was still holding the liquor. He set it down on his night table and put on his sleep shorts. He lay down again, exhausted for some unknown reason, and slipped back into his slumber, carrying with him images of her face. Her beautiful face he could look at every day until the end of days. Yes, she was special unlike any other woman he had ever met. He imagined he would have the sweetest of dreams since he was thinking of her as he sunk into subconscious. He looked forward to another good night's sleep; maybe this time his dreams would be of her.

But luck wouldn't see it his way after all. His dreams took him to another place instead. This one was dark, and he could feel its intensity as though it were happening in real time in the conscious world. In it, it had been dusk, the sun nearly complete in its setting for the night. Creed was in the woods, but the woods had been charred, burned beyond the typical controlled burn. The fire that burned here raged so hot that nothing would ever grow again. The trees and the ground were black from the inferno that has long since been extinguished. He felt brokenhearted as he walked through the blackened forest but couldn't understand why. He just felt a burden of heavy sorrow and anguish beyond relief. Although the burning occurred years before, he could smell the burnt wood of the trees and the ashen earth.

In the distance, he could see the silhouette of a man, hung by his feet from a huge burnt tree. Everything around was crispy, except for the hanging man. He slowly crept toward him to see if he could help or if the swinger was only a body now. As Creed approached him, he could see the man had been disemboweled, bloody and gutted like a prize deer. In all the horrors he had seen while serving on the force, he never saw anything like this. The blow flies already set up house and began their feast of the man's flesh. Creed was repulsed and curious at the same time. Who would do this, he thought. What would someone have to do that was so bad that this would be their punishment? He came in a little closer to examine the scene, and horrible as it was, he was driven by what cause would justify such a horrendous death. Upon inspection of the dead man, he felt like he was being watched and turned in the direction he felt it coming from to see another man standing and watching.

Creed's hair on the back of his neck stood up again in that familiar heebie-jeebies fashion. Not knowing if the tall black man was friend or foe, Creed threw up his hand and waved at the stranger. When the unknown man waved back, Creed assumed him to be friend rather than foe and started to walk toward him. The man then began to go toward Creed, and when he approached, he said something to Creed that he didn't understand.

"I'm sorry, I didn't get that. What'd you say? Creed asked the stranger.

"*Mwen se sou lot bo' a,*" the tall light-skinned black man said again.

Creed was clueless as to what he was saying, but he knew it was the Creole he had heard spoken by the people here.

"Do you speak English? I have no idea what you're trying to tell me, mister," Creed asked him. Now close enough, he could see the man's eyes were blue, and not just any blue eyes but the same pacific blue and shape as his own and Caroline's. This was very surprising to Creed, and his curiosity about who the man was grew tenfold at the sight of his eyes. The Haitian man must've been kin somehow with eyes like that, but Caroline hadn't told him of this relative, if that was what he was. And Creed was pretty sure that he was to some degree. There was something else she would have to tell him about; not that it was neglected, he was sure, perhaps, she just hadn't gotten around to telling him about this one yet. After all, he had just arrived, and there was a lot to know. He just didn't know this, but he would find out when he talked to Caroline again.

He turned to point out the dead man to the Haitian and ask the stranger if he knew who the victim may have been and what had happened to him, although what had happened to him was obvious. But as he started to speak to him, he had disappeared into thin air, like he had never been there at all. And now Creed was alone again with the fly-covered carcass, smelling the foulness that the remains reeked of. Creed couldn't imagine what had happened to him or why; he just kept repeating the words the stranger said in his head, so he wouldn't forget them. He would ask Caroline what it meant later. In the dream, he stood with the company of the deceased for a while longer and then woke up to the sound of a hawk's call. He sat straight up from his sleep in a pouring sweat and a terrified feeling. He could actually smell the charred woods of the forest he had just visited in dreamland, and now awake, he heard the bird's call again. Even though he knew it was just another of his crazy and sometimes morbid dreams, he still felt panicked.

After lying there for a while longer and being nowhere near sleep, he got up. It was four in the morning and still too early for breakfast, so he decided to dress and go out for some fresh air. It had done him some good the previous night; he would give it a shot on this night too. There wasn't anything else to do, and he needed the refreshing air. But first, he wrote down what the words sounded like that the

Haitian had said and slipped the written phrase into his front pocket. He wandered about the property near the house and then made his way to the wooden swing that was by the water's edge. It was built well and sturdy and quite a bit more comfortable than it looked. He sat there for almost a half an hour when he noticed two people coming from around the side of the house.

By the shape of their outlines, it looked to be Caroline and Ray, and he wondered what they were doing up this early. He had hoped he didn't wake them somehow in his wandering.

He could see Caroline was smiling as the two were chatting when they got closer. When they were near, she held up a large cup in her hand, and Creed rose to his feet to receive her offering of coffee. He was glad it wasn't too early for that; he could always use a cup. A fresh cup of coffee always paired well with fresh air.

"Oh, thank you, I appreciate that," he told her as he took it from her hand. She had one of her own in her other hand, as did Ray.

"Good morning, can't sleep?" she asked, but she already knew it was a dream that deemed him to hold company with her at this early hour.

"No, not now. I was actually sleeping pretty good until I had a another dream that didn't make any sense, as usual," Creed replied.

"So why don't you tell me about it?" she asked.

Creed wasn't sure if it would be a good idea to tell her in front of Ray, but she read through it and glanced over at Ray and then back at Creed.

"Your secret's safe with him if that's what you're afraid of," she told him. "Not that you're afraid or anything, but I promise he won't think of you as any weirder than he already does." Then the two rolled in laughter.

"Haha, yeah, yeah, yuck it up, people," Creed said, not finding the hilarity in the joke that they did.

"No, really, it won't bother me, but if you'd rather I leave, I'd understand," Ray commented, still giggling at Caroline's humor.

"You can stay. I don't have anything to hide about the insanity of what my mind comes up with while I'm not paying attention," Creed said.

"Okay, go on, let's hear it," she said with insistence.

Creed began the story of his dream, and right away he noticed they were hanging on to every word he said as he explained it. He told them of the dead man hanging from the burnt tree and of the tall, lean, black man with the same eyes as the ones he shared with Caroline. The more he spoke, the further their jaws dropped, and before he could finish, both Caroline and Ray looked like they had seen more than a ghost with their eyes wide as plates. He wasn't sure why, but he continued right up to the part of hearing that hawk in his dream and again when he woke. It was the same with the smell of the burnt woods in his dream and again when he woke up. Creed took the small piece of paper from his pocket and handed it to Caroline. She sounded it out and asked him if that is what the man said to him, and he nodded to her that it was. He tried to ask about the stranger's eyes, but before he could ask, Caroline and Ray began their own conversation.

"It's Creole for 'I'm on the other side,'" Caroline told him.

"Who's on the other side? I don't know what you mean," Creed asked, lost by the phrase.

"That sounds like Leonard to me," Ray said to her. A deep, curious, whitewash look came over Ray's face. Creed didn't like the expression either. The ghost Creed thought they saw now seemed more like a poltergeist instead. He wasn't sure who Leonard was, but it didn't seem good.

"That is Leonard. It could be no other. The eyes give it away, ya know?" Caroline stated.

"Yeah, I know. What do ya think it means?" Ray asked her with a concerned tone.

"Who's Leonard?" Creed asked to either of them who would answer first. He needed to know who they were talking about since it was him dreaming of someone that was a total stranger to him, but clearly they knew who he was.

"I think it means that Leonard is dead. I think he's died. I know he has, I feel it now," she told Ray.

"Ya think so?" Ray asked in disbelief.

"Who's Leonard?" Creed asked a second time.

"I do, I'll call and find out. If he has, I'll send flowers and a nice wreath for his burial. I'll need you to pay out his funds to his family," Caroline told Ray.

"Yeah, sure, consider it done," Ray replied. "I'll do it this morning when their banks open to do the transfer. That way I know it's guaranteed. I'll give you the confirmation number and receipt for it when it's done."

"Good, I know his family will appreciate it, but I'll call first to be certain," Caroline said to Ray.

"What the hell? I'm right here, I know you hear me. Who's Leonard, and why am I dreaming of him? One of you needs to tell me something, damn it." Creed demanded.

"Easy there, Creed. No need to get your jockeys in a wad," Caroline snapped. She never was one to be demanded of.

"Well then, don't ignore me. I don't like it," Creed snapped back at her. "Now who the hell is Leonard? "

Ray and Caroline gave each other a long stare, and then he told her, "You didn't tell him about Carla yet, did you? You couldn't have, or he would know what he dreamed of." Ray looked at her hard as though he had told her not to bullshit him with his eyes instead of his words.

Caroline drew in a deep breath and then let out a long sigh and said, "No. No, I haven't, but I was going to."

"Well, I think now is the time, don't you? Like you always say, go ahead, put it out on the table." Ray's tone sounded as though he were scolding Caroline for not being as forthcoming as she should have been about her sister.

She was a part of their lives at one time, and she shouldn't be omitted from any conversation that ever bore her name.

"Is somebody going to answer me because now you're just pissing me off." Creed demanded again.

"Oh my God, yes, Creed, for God's sake, I'll tell you. Leonard is an extremely distant relative. He's a direct descendant of our own ancestors from the days when an owner would take his slave women to bed. That's why his eyes are the same. I had to send Leonard away back to Haiti many years ago," Caroline began to say.

"Why? Was it him that hung that man?" Creed asked, eager to know what had happened.

"Yes, let me finish and you'll understand. Well, maybe you'll understand," Caroline said. "That man that was hung was named Billy Marcel. He had affections for my sister that he expressed after Patrick's plane went down. Carla was missing her husband and had no interest in Billy, but he wouldn't take no for an answer since Patrick wasn't around to halt Billy's pursuit of her. He thought she should have fallen to her knees over him, considering there wasn't a slew of suitors lined up to take Patrick's place. There wasn't a slew of them because she didn't allow it; she only had love for Patrick. She complained to me one morning that the previous night, Billy was peeping in at her. There had already been many complaints about him, but that was the final straw for me. I told him to pack up his things and that Leonard would be taking him back to the mainland."

"Well, he didn't make it. Why?" Creed inquired.

"Because after he packed up and was heading to the house from this cottage near the south end, he caught Carla alone. She had been picking blackberries that grew wild in the woods on the southeast side of the island. She ran but tripped on some ground vines and fell into some palmettos where baby rattlesnakes were nested. She was struck more times than could be counted and had enough venom in her to kill a horse. She tried to run again, but she didn't get far before her muscles started to seize. She had to know then that she wouldn't make it. Carla was smart enough to know that nobody survives that many poisonous strikes, no way. That didn't matter to Billy; he had her right where he wanted her. Helpless and vulnerable, he took the chance to have his way with her. And her convulsing didn't deter him one bit either. He continued to rape Carla even after her life had left her." Caroline's own words had her choking up. She swallowed hard, sipped her coffee, and picked up where she had left off. Ray just sat and listened; he would make sure Caroline left nothing out.

"It was Leonard that caught up with Billy, and Billy swinging from the tree was the aftermath of what he committed. Such a heinous act warrants a heinous punishment, does it not? And Leonard carried out his own form of punishment because he found him first. I was angry at Leonard for the vengeance he sought, but in his thinking, he thought he was doing me a favor by taking Billy out. That way, I wouldn't have to kill Billy myself."

"Why would you have to kill him? Is there no other way?" Creed asked.

"No, Creed, there's not. That's what I meant by judge, jury, and executioner. It was my place to deal with Billy, not Leonard's. I know his intentions were well meant, but the road to hell is paved with good intentions. When Leonard showed Ray and I his body, Ray told Leonard to cut him down, and I said to let him hang as a warning to everyone else that we were not to be reckoned with. Anyway, because of what he had done, distant relative or not, I had to deal with him. I thought it to be best to send him home for good. We continued his salary so he could have a good life in Haiti." She paused for a moment and then continued, "It was either send him away or kill him. It's my position to do to him what he had done to another. But the truth is, I couldn't see that any good would come from killing Leonard, and I wasn't going to. So I sent him away."

As hard as it was to believe, Creed could rationalize what she meant. It did make sense to him, as crazy as it sounded. It was better to send him away than to have brought him harm. Although there was a lot more to the "position" she had offered than he was really prepared for, this was heavy for Creed, and he would have to reassess what he had gotten himself into. Then he noticed the sky had turned overcast before the light of dawn. The clouds hid what moonlight was still left, but it didn't seem like the clouds would release their captive water and rain, just the grayness. Ray kept a watchful eye on them and on Caroline, as if she were the special ed kid that was missing her helmet that day. Creed didn't recognize the purpose of Ray's attentiveness, or even that Ray had been paying such close attention to her. But he would later come to learn why Ray did so.

"How did the woods catch fire?" Creed asked her.

"I set the fire to burn and set into ash what had happened and to burn out any more nesting snakes in that palmetto-infested part of the woods. I've always hated that section because it was so thick with them. Now a palmetto will never grow there again, nor will anything else for that matter," she said.

"I see," was all Creed could say.

"Do you? Do you really?" Caroline asked sincerely.

"Yeah, I think I do, but why did he come to me in my dream? Why didn't he just come to you?" Creed asked with that look of deep curiosity, bewildered by all he had just learned.

"That's a good question, and I don't have the answer, but he did get his message delivered through you, didn't he?" she asked.

"Yeah, I suppose he did," Creed replied.

Just then, headlights of a big box truck could be seen coming up the small drive to the back of the house, and the diesel motor's hearty roar increased the closer it got.

"Who the hell is that at this hour?" Creed alerted them.

Ray laughed and said, "They're for you. That's all of your stuff. I told you it would be here by sunrise. Looks like I'm ahead of schedule. Chalk one up for me."

Creed had nearly forgotten about his belongings with the whirlwind of things going on. His jaw dropped, and then he said, "You gotta be shittin' me!" He couldn't believe Ray managed to pull that all together overnight.

"Nah, I wouldn't shit ya. You're my favorite turd. Now where do you want it?" Ray said, and he and Caroline burst into deep belly laughs. Even Creed had to laugh after all. That Ray fella was pretty good to get it all here overnight.

"I'm not sure yet," Creed answered. He hadn't given any thought as to where to put anything.

"Don't sweat it. I'll have them park it, and then it can be taken care of later. I'll go ahead and give them a ride back." Then he stood to walk back to the house.

"Hey, Ray, thanks. I appreciate you getting that done for me. I owe you one," Creed said.

"You're welcome, but you owe me nothin'," Ray said as he looked back with a smile. He threw up one hand and said, "I'm out, later ya'll."

"See ya," Caroline said, and then she turned to Creed.

"So you got any plans for your day off today?" she asked him.

With a huge grin, he replied, "As a matter of fact, I do. I'm spending the day at the lagoon with Megan."

"I thought so," she began to say when he suddenly interrupted her.

"Oh, did she tell you?" he asked, wondering if Megan was already awake this morning.

"No, but I pulled out a basket and a pair of clippers for you. They're on the kitchen table, and there's a vase on the counter by the sink for you to put them in. The gardens are that way in case you didn't know," she said and then pointed in the direction where he was to go to cut flowers for his date.

Creed snickered, finding it funny that she knew something that no one had told her and how she knew he would be picking flowers for her as well.

"Thanks, I remember you said gardenias and lavender," he said.

"And anything else you want to throw in there, she loves them all. Those just happen to be her favorites." Caroline advised him.

"I should probably get to that then," he said, acknowledging the sun to rise soon, and he wanted to be ready.

"Yep, you probably should," she replied. "You guys have fun today."

As Creed stood up, he said, "We should. Thanks and I'll see you later."

"See ya."

From the Fresh Spring Waters
Runs a River Forlorn

As the sun rose, Creed meandered around the gardens, snipping the finest flowers he could find—big, fat, heavily fragrant blooms everywhere the eye could see. So strong were their aromas that a blind man could see their beauty in his imagination. Creed never considered himself a garden kind of guy, but he found he loved being in the garden, especially cutting her favorites. He liked the way everything had its own unique smell, mostly sweet like the lavender and gardenias. The lilies weren't overpowering, but they were big pretty flowers, and Caroline said that Megan would like them too. He cut some goldenrod, snapdragons, and even some magnolias from the trees that border the gardens because he thought they smelled nice. Creed knew he had cut too many, but he would think of something to do with the extras. He would just have to be a little creative, that's all.

He brought his loaded basket into the kitchen and went to work. He arranged the large vase and filled it with the tall bright flowers. Then he thought about what he would do with the gardenias and magnolias. He remembered there was a table with a mirror above it a few feet from her door. He looked around the kitchen and saw a swallow glass bowl that would do nicely. He put a little water in it and placed the sweet blooms perfectly. Creed was a little proud of himself; he didn't know he had it in him to make floral arrangements. He couldn't help but laugh out loud at himself, and it felt good to be able to do that again. He carried the dish to the table by her door, set it down, and turned it until he thought it was just right. Then he thought he should start packing the picnic lunch that he told her he would do. He was so excited with anticipation and looking forward to the day when it suddenly dawned on him— he had forgotten to ask Megan what she would like for the picnic.

Creed realized there was much work to do with the delivery of his possessions. But Caroline said everyone had the day off, and he had a date he wasn't going to miss, come hell or high water. He would have to put all work on hold for now. As he entered the kitchen, he thought he would make sandwiches, although he didn't know if she would like what he made. There on the table sat an enormous picnic basket. He thought Caroline must have pulled it out for him, like she did for the flowers. He smiled and walked over to pick it up. It was heavy, so he set it back down to see what was inside. Just as he opened the flap, Caroline walked in. Upon seeing the cornucopia of food inside, Creed looked up at her.

"You did this? Wow, there's a lot of food in there. Is that a bottle of wine?" Creed asked. The night before, Megan drank brandy. He didn't know she liked wine as well.

"Yeah, I made a few ham sandwiches, the way Megan likes them, and there are grapes, strawberries, and pears in there too. She likes fruit and that bottle is a good one from my private cellar. It's a 1951 dark red. She also likes that," Caroline informed him, as if she were reading the special of the day from the menu.

"I…I don't know what to say. Thank you, I appreciate you doing that. I had no idea what I was going to make for her. Did you say you have a private wine cellar?" he asked, surprised. He hadn't known anyone to have a wine cellar before; it struck him odd.

Caroline laughed out loud. "Yes, I did and? So I like a fine wine from time to time, what's wrong with that?" she asked him in a slightly defensive tone yet with a smile.

Creed thought about it for a second and then replied, "Well, nothing, I suppose. I just never knew anyone with their own wine cellar. If that's what you like, it's okay by me."

"Thanks for your permission," she said and laughed harder this time. Creed laughed too. It was not what he meant, but she made a joke of it.

"Anyway, I have about an hour until I meet her. I should probably get a shower first. Thank you again for the lunch and wine," Creed told her.

"No problem, I want you two to have a good time today, all right? And if you look in the bottom drawer of your armoire, you'll find some swimming trunks in there along with a few other clothes. They should fit since all your stuff is still in the truck."

Creed felt more welcome there in that moment than he had ever felt anywhere in his life. She was really looking out for him, and she didn't have to; she just did. Even with all the bad he was learning, he was gaining a fond appreciation for Caroline. He liked it here, and with everything that wasn't good, this place and its residents were good for him, especially Megan. He couldn't believe everyone here was so good to him, but he could accept that for a change.

"Caroline, I'd like to thank you for everything. Your kindness means a lot to me," he said in a gentle tone. "It really does."

She smiled softly and said, "Don't overthink it. Just have some relaxing fun, you both deserve it." Then she turned and walked out.

Creed made good use of the last hour he would have to wait to see Megan. He showered, shaved, popped two pills, and found the swimming trunks. Again, Caroline was right—they fit him like a glove. He took the vase of flowers he arranged and set them on the table and then knocked on her door to see if she was ready to go or if she may want some breakfast before they went to the lagoon. She swung it open with a nearly eaten English muffin she was holding and chewed on the rest. Megan's green eyes lit up at the sight of the huge bouquet he held.

"Oh, wow, they're beautiful, Creed. Thank you, but how did you know these are my favorites?" she gushed.

"I got lucky, I guess," he replied, thinking how helpful Caroline's information had been.

"It looks to me like I'm the lucky one. So it was you who put the bowl of flowers outside my room? Because I love them, I like opening my door to the smell of fresh flowers. Oh, please come in," she said and stepped out of the way to allow him in. She shoved the rest of the English muffin in her mouth and took the vase from his hands, gently caressing them as she did so.

"Did you eat anything yet?" she asked.

"Yeah, I had a couple of leftover biscuits," he said.

"Are you ready then?" she asked him.

"I'm ready if you're ready," he answered, grinning like the Cheshire cat. Then she kissed him on his cheek and thanked him again. *Oh, it would be a good day, indeed, if it's starting like that*, he thought. Megan picked up a bag, which Creed quickly took and carried for her. She smiled and blushed a little; he was being a gentleman, and she really liked that. She certainly didn't meet a lot of those on the island.

"We'll take my jeep," she said. He followed her out of her room and into the grand hallway, thinking about how nice she looked. She was beautiful, even from behind. She had on a white cotton button-up shirt with a navy blue bikini top on underneath. He thought about how good she probably looked in it when she took the shirt off. And her shorts were a dark blue denim, in which she filled out rather well. Brickhouse, no doubt about it. She had a blue velvet hair tie around her wrist, which he assumed was for later, for now her long blond hair flowed with every step she took. Not to mention, she had a saucy little bounce, and yet she seemed to float as she walked. Creed was glad to be behind her because he couldn't hide his proud grin, proud to be spending time with a girl like that and proud that she wanted to spend her time with a guy like him. Little did Creed know that she felt the very same way about him. She found Creed to be funny and charming. Megan thought he was smart and very handsome, and what girl wouldn't want a man like him?

He put her bag in the backseat and then settled into the front passenger seat. She pulled her hair back with the hair tie she had on her wrist and then cranked the engine and put it in gear. They talked on the way, and she asked Creed if he had been to the spring yet. He said he hadn't, and she promised to take him there when they left the beach.

"It's a good place to wash off the saltwater from the lagoon," she told him. "And it's good for the skin." Then she said something else that caught him completely off guard.

"You know about what happened to my mother, don't you? Aunt Caroline told you, didn't she?" she asked him.

"I do know, I won't lie to you. But it was because I dreamed of the destruction of the fallout afterward. I thought Caroline would know what it meant, and she did. That's what I know," Creed replied, keeping secret the details of her mother's murder. He didn't feel she needed to know that he knew, but he would be receptive if she felt the need to talk about it.

"I'm asking so it doesn't come up again. I know the basics of what happened to the parents that adopted me, but I choose not to know the specifics because I believe it'll flood my mind with more grief than I already have by losing them in the first place. I don't have the gifts you and Aunt Caroline have, and I do better moving forward than I do dwelling in the past, and that's how I deal with it every day. So I'd rather not talk about it, if you don't mind. I'm happier that way," Megan explained. She hoped he would understand and not pry too much.

That was fine with Creed. If that was how she preferred it, that was good by him. He certainly wasn't going to make her talk about it, and in the same respect, he would rather not talk about killing that teenager who ran amuck.

Hopefully, it wouldn't come up because, like her, he didn't wish to discuss particular subjects either.

"That's not a problem, we don't have to," Creed replied with that soft understanding in his voice and expression.

"Thanks, Creed," she said.

He thought the sound of his name had never been sweeter. The way it came out of her mouth when she spoke it was like his name was being made into a musical note. She reached over and squeezed his hand, and he held hers for a moment before letting go. He didn't want to, but he didn't want to come on too strong either. That always scares a girl away. Her hands were soft and fit perfectly inside his. He liked the way it felt, and he hoped it wouldn't be long until he could hold her hand again. It didn't take too long to get to the beach he and Caroline previously visited. It was a perfect day for it too, and the tide was coming in. There were no real waves, just the rise of the water level at high tide. Then they set up with a beach blanket, a few towels, and the picnic basket in a spot that Megan thought was the best spot in the sand.

"Are ya a good swimmer, Creed?" she asked, flirty with her big green eyes looking up at him. The sunlight in her eyes made them beam, almost glow. He wondered if she knew how naturally pretty she was—no makeup and her hair pulled back to expose her whole face, her perfect skin soft and smooth and warmed in the sun.

"I'm decent. I know how to if that's what you mean. Why?" he asked. The lagoon was safe enough for anyone, he thought.

"Well, there's a rope I'd like to swing on up that way about a half a mile. You can only do it when the tide's coming in because the current is so strong. It will bring us right back here. It's not so much swimming if you can float your way back. Can you swim that far?" she asked excitedly.

Creed could see how much she wanted to go, but he also could sense that she wanted him to go with her. He was no fool; he was going, and he could swim and float. By God, he would not miss out on that. Not only was she a beauty but she was also fun and so easy to be with. It was hard to believe someone like her was real.

"You're damn right I can swim that far, let's go." He was up for her challenge, and he gave her his own flirty smile.

"This will be fun," she said with a big smile that made her eyes dance. Then she began to unbutton the white shirt she was wearing over her bathing suit top. Creed shifted his eyes away to be polite and not gawk at her like he really wanted to. He would be a gentleman if it killed him, and he thought it just might. She pulled the shirt off and tossed it down on the blanket, and then she motioned with her hand for him to follow her. He couldn't help but notice how the sides of her breasts protruded from her bikini top. Not too much but just enough that he could see her perfectly shaped flesh. He knew he was in trouble; she stirred something in him he hadn't known before, and he liked it. He liked what he was feeling for her, even if it was all fantasy in his mind; he liked it. He never felt that raw chemistry until now, and that in itself was something altogether different than any other experience he'd had in the past.

He followed her along the path and up the hill. The half mile went fast since he was watching his step and her backside, mostly her backside. He couldn't help himself—he was under her spell, whatever bewitching spell it was. It wasn't all about her looks, it was about her. She was so easy to be with. He was comfortable around her, yet he had that nervous boyhood, first crush thing going on too. That he couldn't understand, but it didn't change the fact he wanted to be with her in every way he could. Creed wanted to know all there was to know about her. They reached the spot where the rope swing was, and they looked out over the water. Megan was right—the current ran swift through the bight and that rope dropped off into it. As hard as it rushed in, he could see why you wouldn't do it with the tide going out; that would sweep you out to sea.

"What do ya think? You up for it?" she asked him, sounding more like she was daring than asking.

Creed was up for it, all right. And that wasn't all he was up for. But he would behave himself. He didn't want to scare "sweet thing" off.

"Oh, yeah," he said, nodding his head. "Who's going first?"

"Want to go together? We'll cannonball, it'll be fun," she said.

"You're on," he said. "How do you want to do this?" he asked, not sure of the best way for two people to swing out at once or if it was even a good idea.

"Grab a knot and hold on until we're all the way out. Then let go and get into your cannonball. The current's gonna take us all the way in," she explained.

"All right, let's do this," he said, readying himself for the thrill of dropping the sixteen feet or so into the fast-moving water.

She pulled the rope over to them, and they gripped the knots that would best steady themselves on the outward swing. She had Creed reposition one of his arms so as to not black her eye with his elbow on the ride out. They both had a good laugh, and then she asked if he was sure he wanted to do this, and he quickly said he was.

"Wait," he said. "I want to ask you something first."

"What? You're not gonna chicken out, are you?" she asked. He couldn't have cut it any shorter. She was ready to swing out when he stopped her.

"No chicken here, I just want to know something. You said you don't have a gift, but you do. How do you charm those bees like you do?" He wanted to know this since he first saw her in the grove.

She smiled wide again and then touched his face. "I'm not charming them exactly." She laughed. "The bees are attracted to my pheromones, that's all it is."

"The bees aren't the only ones," he told her. That was a hint she would have to get, he thought. And she definitely got it loud and clear. She let go of a knot she held and placed her hand on the nape of his neck. She leaned closer into him, pressing her body against his, and kissed him. He didn't see it coming, but since her lips were on his, he would continue to kiss her back as long as she'd allow it. Her lips were warm and sweet on his, and he liked how soft they felt. Then she slipped her tongue between his lips to kiss him deeper. Her tongue was like warm, wet velvet, and her kiss made him feel like it was the first kiss he ever had. Her skin against his had him excited, and he could feel himself swell. He hoped she wouldn't feel him rise or, worse, notice the pulsating throb she was giving him. He wasn't sure he could hide it much longer when she pulled away from him and smiled. She let go of his neck and grabbed the knot she had a hold of before. She nodded her head as the cue to swing out, and they went out together over the water.

They let go and dropped simultaneously; however, Megan's cannonball was perfect in form, while Creed's was not. He did something more of a half ball, half flop because his mind and body were still caught up in the kiss she had given him rather than his cannonball skills. As they came up from under the water, Megan was laughing and having the best time. Creed laughed at hearing her laugh. It was good to hear, and he knew there wasn't enough of that in his life. They floated in with the current, and before they made it all the way back, Megan swam over to Creed. He took her hand, and she floated closer, but Creed couldn't take it anymore. He pulled her through the water until she was within inches, and then he took her in his arms. Face-to-face, he held her tight, her breasts pressed into his chest. He kissed her deep, needing to feel her tongue again. She certainly wasn't pulling away, and he couldn't believe this gorgeous woman was letting him put his tongue in her mouth. He wondered where else she would let him put his tongue or what else she would let him slip into her mouth. He felt the hard throb come again, and he couldn't stop it.

As much as he wanted her, he knew it was too soon for any kind of physical relations. They had only met a couple of days ago, and he didn't want to ruin it by rushing it, but he couldn't control what she was doing to him. His desire to be inside of her was more intense than he had ever felt for any woman. It was so strong that the throb was beginning to hurt. He hadn't been with a woman, nor had he relieved himself for some time, and now he was paying for it. He would pay whatever price as long as he could keep kissing her and feeling her breasts with her rock hard nipples pressing against him. He was holding her by the small of her back when she wrapped her legs around him and kissed his neck and then his ear. He pulled away from it, and she was surprised.

"I'm sorry. What did I do?" she asked. She thought he might like that, but she must've been mistaken.

"God, nothing. I swear, you didn't do anything wrong. I'm, um, I'm getting too worked up. The ear thing, it drives me crazy, and I'm already near the brink. I promise, you did nothing wrong. I just need to control myself, that's all," Creed explained.

"The brink? What is the brink for you?" she asked.

"The brink is the point in which I want to snatch off that suit and take you. I wouldn't do that because it's wrong, but I can't say I don't want to," Creed told her.

"Oh. Well, if I promise not to do that anymore, can I still kiss you?" she asked.

"By all means, yes, you can kiss me anytime you want to," he said.

"Good because I like kissing you," she said.

"Then come kiss me, girl," he said, smiling, and she happily obliged. They kissed and floated all the way back to where they set everything up on the beach. When they made it beachside, they didn't get out of the water right away but swam around some instead, talking and getting to know each other better. Then they lay in the sand just beneath the water. The tide was beginning to go out, and it was warm as bath water. Creed was saying something when she rolled over on top of him and kissed him.

She stopped for a moment and then asked him, "Am I being too forward? I'm not good at this kind of thing, and I don't want to be too forward."

Creed looked at her and smiled. He was the luckiest man on the planet for her to be hot for him. He grabbed her just below her arms and rolled her over on her back in the shallow water. He kissed her deeply as he climbed on top of her. Then he stopped and looked into her eyes.

"You could never be too forward. But I do promise to be a gentleman and respect you. I'm not going to do anything out of the way," he told her.

"I didn't think you would. You've been very sweet to me," she said.

"That's all I want to be. And I hope you let me be sweet to you some more. I admit I really like being with you, and my desire to have you is overwhelming, but I will behave myself," he said.

"There's something about you that is making me want you too. I've never been like this, and that's why I didn't want to come on too strong and scare you away," she said.

"That's what I was afraid of. I didn't want to scare you off either." He interrupted her.

They both laughed at the other for their same way of thinking, and he realized he was liking her more and more.

"Well, I'm glad you haven't run away because I feel something with you I haven't felt before," she said.

"Oh, yeah? What's that?" he asked. He knew there was no way she would say the L-word. They didn't know each other that well yet, and if it was, that just might scare him off.

"Maybe I shouldn't say this, but I feel like I can tell you anything, Creed, like you're my best friend or something. I just feel like I can talk to you. Anyway, you're the only man I ever wanted to give myself to. Not yet, but I do at some point, and I want it to be you when I do," she told him.

Creed tried to process what she had just said. Was she saying what he thought she was saying? he wondered. It's not possible as beautiful as she was; he must've heard her wrong.

"I'm sorry, are you saying, um, that, um? I'm trying to follow you, but are you saying…?" He was trying to ask.

"Yes, I'm saying I've haven't been with a man before, but when I do, I want it to be you. You do something to me that's unlike anything I can imagine," she said.

He could only look at her with a blank, stupid stare. Creed couldn't believe his ears. This unbelievably hot woman, who was actually hot for him as well, was a virgin, and it was him she wanted to give herself to. He thought he should pinch himself, but he could feel her in his arms—this was real. She was real, all of her. How did he get so lucky? What the hell was going on in the universe that all the planets aligned? He thought maybe he was about to be struck by lightning or the sky would fall. His luck couldn't be this good.

Creed assured her that it was okay, and if it was meant to be, it would happen eventually. He suggested they eat something; after all, they spent most of the morning swimming and making out, mostly making out. They both had raging chemistry for one another that neither could deny. But they needed nourishment, and the wine sounded like a fine idea to them both. Besides, he really needed a distraction from her. It was early afternoon, and they made plans for later that evening to see each other. However, Creed still had a loaded truck to take care of, and he was wanting to get as much done as he could before dinner so he could spend the rest of the night with Megan—unless, of course, Caroline needed him for something. If so, hopefully he wouldn't be long. After their lunch, they packed up all they had brought and then headed down the limestone road toward the spring where they could rinse off the saltwater that soaked into their skin. All Creed could think about was the dream girl beside him and what a perfect day it had been with her. He could do this every day, especially the kissing and touching part. Although he wanted to touch more, he would be happy for now with what he did touch.

Megan pulled the jeep along the side of the road and turned the key off. She told Creed the spring was just a short distance down the path she had parked by. She told him to go ahead without her and that she would catch up. She said she "needed a minute," which Creed quickly discovered was code for needing to use the restroom where there wasn't one. He knew she was definitely his dream girl now. He never thought about it until right now, but for a girl to pee behind a tree and not complain about it was the girl made for him. Not griping and no shame in "when a girl's gotta go, a girl's gotta go." What an awesome woman, he thought. Up the path, he could hear running water and knew he was getting close. Then he thought he saw something through the trees. He could tell it was a person standing out near the mouth of the spring but wasn't sure who it was at first. He soon realized it was Caroline standing in the water. Her white shirt in the bright sun made it appear that there was an aura encircling her in glowing white light. Creed thought she looked angelic.

He called out to her, but Caroline couldn't hear him for the flowing water from the spring down the rocks and into a wide creek. However, she knew he was there. She just wasn't finished yet. He walked out into the water to see if she was all right since she wasn't replying to him. Caroline would answer when she was done and only when she was done. As he waded out into the cool fresh water, he continued calling out to her, but she just stood motionless. With her back to him, he couldn't see her face. There was no expression for him to see, to know if she was okay. When he was within a few feet of her, she turned her head to the side, the same way she did in the corridor. He thought she finally heard him, but she didn't need to hear him to know he was there. She would finish her prayer before she replied.

"Yes, Creed, I'm okay." Her response was overdue.

"Well, why are you standing out here like that? In the water?" he asked, concerned she may be upset about something.

Caroline's head may have been turned to see only half, but he could see in that half something tortured and pained.

"I was baptized right here in this very spot when I was only ten years old, but I understood. Everyone I've ever loved, I've lost right here on this island. And I come here to pray, to tell them how much they are missed and still loved. I've cried a river for my loved ones, more tears than all the water that runs here, and it doesn't bring them back. It only means that I'll see them in another time and another place," Caroline explained.

Creed wasn't sure what to say or what to do. He stood quietly for a moment, thinking that since she was in prayer, he should disappear and then asked her, "Would you rather be alone right now?"

"I would, thank you," she replied.

Creed said nothing more; he simply turned and made his way to dry land. He looked up and saw Megan coming to the water's edge, all the while remaining silent. When he walked up to her, she whispered to him that she didn't think Caroline would be there yet, but that she did come here sometimes; she just usually came later in the day.

Creed said it was all right and that they should probably go back to the house and take showers instead. Megan said she couldn't agree more, and they headed down the path again.

On This Day a Hard Storm Brews

Creed arrived back at his suite to find most of his things had been moved in for him. To his surprise, his clothes were put away in drawers and the closet. A note left by Ray said he had the moving guys do it for him, and the rest was in a storage facility there on the premises, so he could settle in a little easier. Well, that was one less thing he had to do himself; therefore, he would have to owe him one. Creed wasn't sure how he could express his appreciation, but he would try to think of something. If he couldn't come up with an idea of his own, he could always ask Caroline. She knew Ray the best and would know what he liked. He might just go straight to her and save himself the trouble. She seemed to have all the answers anyway. Creed would need to do something really nice for him.

He showered and readied himself for dinner and time shared with Megan. Nothing was mentioned throughout the meal about Caroline standing in that spring earlier that afternoon. He didn't understand fully, but he did get some of it. He did understand that all people are different and react to things differently because of it. It's what makes each of us individuals unique in our own right, the way we were made. He hadn't known all that Caroline had been through that made her who she was, but same went for him and all of his trials and tribulations as well. He had come to learn not to judge others, for he too had been judged. That much he had figured out about Caroline. She had her own deep perception of things that only she understood in its full capacity. Even if she explained it and he got it in depth, it still would not be seen for all it was. She was sagacious and didn't hide it or deny that she was. That too was one of the extraordinary characteristics that made her unique, special, from others. We all have that "thing" that makes us different—hers being the id part of her brain that was wide open much like Creed's wildly wicked dreams.

It was another fine meal, come and gone. Caroline talked to Creed for a few minutes before she excused herself to take care of some other matters. She mentioned she had business to attend to, and then she would be spending some time with Ray. Megan had a forty-five-minute class, and then she would be free. So he took advantage of the time and got around to listening to the CD Ray had given him and had a drink while he waited for her. It was nice to have someone to be waiting on. Back in his room, he put the CD in and poured a drink. He thought he better take a pill or two to calm his nerves for the evening. As the music played, the words to the song Ray said could have been written about Caroline made Creed stop it and play it over. Each word of it described just who she was and why, like the guys who wrote it knew her personally.

It seemed crazy, but the lyrics made perfect sense to Creed—it was what Ray was trying to tell him about Caroline. So she talked to ghosts and the ones that left her behind. He thought about the times he talked to his deceased mother; not knowing if she could hear him, he talked to her anyway. He loved and missed her so much, and he realized it was a normal thing to do when losing a loved one. In Caroline's case, she did so on a higher level. She did feel left behind by the ones she loved, and much of her time was spent on the 'dead and dreaming,' waiting for that day to be back with them and to be in Luke's arms again. Although it seemed like she was a lonely middle-aged woman, she was not. She lost most of her family and never having children with the man she loved it would appear that way. However, she most appreciated the bonds of friendship and family that wasn't blood. Those relationships are what meant the most to her.

The next track played, and Creed got the creepy feeling again with the hair standing up on the back of his neck. Ray was spot-on with the lyrics to the second track. It did sound like Creed and the way he was along with the why. He had been waiting, and now the next great thing had come his way when he was beginning to think all great things for him were long gone. It was hard for him to believe all the good happening to him in light of all the recent bad. He imagined that was why he decided to stay. He would take all the good he could get. And the people here were comfortable with him, and some, like Ray and Caroline, somehow seemed to know him. It was a change to be with those you could be close with, the kind he could have a lifelong relationship with. Creepy or not, he liked it regardless. For a moment, he thought he could spend the rest of his life here. He had some peace here in spite of the creepiness that crawled up his spine.

When Megan's class was over, she knocked on his door and asked him if he would like to go for a walk along the water's edge. He would have happily walked to hell on broken glass if that was what she wanted to do. Besides, it was a good evening for it—the sun was setting, and the breeze kept the bugs away. Walking by the sea, he held her hand, and he couldn't help thinking something was wrong with her to want to be with a guy like him. He certainly wasn't going to ask her; he was delighted to spend any moment he could with her. In the twilight, they strolled through the gardens hand in hand. Megan would stop and smell some of the flowers; she was beautiful with a bloom beneath her nose. It wasn't a scene he saw for a long time— someone taking the time to stop and smell the roses, along with a variety of others. He grew fonder of these gardens and of her with each passing minute. He truly loved this island and all it had to offer.

The evening turned to night, and it was late as they sat on her back porch. In rocking chairs, they talked the night away, which makes up for all the time they spent making out earlier that morning. Creed thought he should be turning in since everyone had to work the next day. He began to excuse himself for the night and intended to make plans to see her again the following day when she interrupted his "good nights." She asked him to stay just to hold her until she fell asleep. Before he could answer, she apologized if that was too bold of a thing to ask. Creed told her it wasn't and that he'd like that. She proceeded to tell him she wanted to know what it was like to fall asleep in his arms with her head on his chest, listening to his heartbeat. It was something she always wanted to do, and with Creed, she felt like she needed to, like she needed to feel him.

He would, without a doubt, hold her all that she wanted. He was happy to be the man she wanted to be held by, the man she needed. She changed into a pair of silky pajama shorts with a matching camisole and climbed into the huge soft bed where in the middle he was waiting for her. He stretched his arm out to her, and she laid her head on his chest. She listened to the thumping inside. Wrapped in his arms was heaven on earth for her and a memory she would never forget. It would be etched inside her mind until her last breath. Creed pulled her chin up, kissed her softly, and told her good night. She smiled and said the same and then thanked him. He told her no thanks was needed and pulled her closer to him. While he held her, he thought about how so much had changed for the better in only a few days. Only a few days ago, he thought about pulling the trigger, ending it all. Silently, he thanked God or whoever was listening to his thoughts for still being here for him, for giving him hope. Soon her breathing would change, and she would be in dreamland.

After she slipped off and picked up a small gentle snore, Creed thought he would lie there and hold her all night. It was the best feeling he had in sometime, and he didn't want it to end. She had a Mona Lisa smile on her face as she slept, and he imagined he could look at her all night like that. She was perfect, even when she snored—yes, his dream girl indeed. But as he lay there thinking about it, he thought maybe it would be best if he snuck out without waking her. He was already having difficulty keeping his hands off of her and not ripping her clothes off to ravage her perfect body, her perfect flesh. It would be so much worse when he woke up in the morning next to her with a raging hard-on and not being able to do anything about it. At least, if he were in his own bed, he could do something about it if need be. Furthermore, he thought maybe she would miss him if he wasn't there in the morning. It might make her want him more than she already did. He didn't want to let her go, but after a while, he slid out from under her and put a pillow under her head. Then he went back to his own room wishing he had stayed.

Morning came sooner than expected, and Creed woke to a salute from down below. She was killing him, he thought. He decided a cold shower would be best for this situation. If that didn't work, he'd take care of it himself. After that, he would get food, starved once again. As he was dressing, he smelled breakfast cooking and hurried to get some of the bacon he could almost taste in the air. Breakfast was good, but no Megan.

Soon Caroline entered the kitchen and asked Bea if she had come in to eat, and Bea told her she was already out in the grove so she could finish up early. Caroline and Creed thought that he may be the reason to get through with work as soon as possible, but neither said anything about it. He asked Caroline what she would like for him to do today, and she replied by telling him he would need to go with Ray to the storehouse and get some supplies. She said he should get whatever he may need as well while they were there, and Creed said he would, although he didn't need much.

Not long after she gave him the instructions for how he was to spend his day, Ray came into the kitchen and piled up a plate of food. He asked if Creed would be ready to go after he ate, and Creed said he would be. Caroline passed Ray a list of the things she needed for him to get because she had some things she had to do and wouldn't be free until early afternoon at best. Ray took the list and tucked it into one of his pockets, never missing a beat shoving his mouth full. Both men had eaten their food as if they were starving, and it was their first meal in months. It wasn't far from looking like pigs at a trough. Caroline made no mention of it because sometimes a person just has to eat. When their bellies were full, the two headed out the back door, while Ray yelled back at Caroline that he would see her later, and then they were soon cruising down the east road toward the storehouse.

Ray made small talk about the weather and such at first and then asked Creed if he had a chance to listen to the music Ray passed on to him. He said he had but that he didn't know how Ray was so good at having someone pegged as quickly as he did, especially him. He understood Caroline because Ray had known her for decades, but Creed he had just met. He told Ray that was a pretty cool talent he had for doing that. Ray explained to Creed that although Caroline was very different from regular, everyday people, she was, nonetheless, one of the good people to know. She was just strange to most folks. Creed said it didn't matter; he liked Caroline, and she was family at that. He wanted to know her and her oddities. Ray told him she couldn't let go of the ones she loved; it was just her nature. Creed understood—he had a nature of his own.

Then Ray said something that threw Creed into left field. Out of the blue, Creed didn't see it coming.

"Caroline has expressed to me that you had an interest in what I may know about Danny Rolling. I don't like to talk about it, but I believe if you want to have a good rapport with someone, you should have the ability to just ask. So what would you like to know?" Ray asked, opening the door wide for Creed to ask anything he wanted to.

This was an opportunity that would come but once in a lifetime, if at all. It was Creed's chance, and he was going to take it like all the other opportunities that have presented themselves in the last few days.

"Wow, really? I understand if you don't want to talk about it. I respect that," Creed said, thinking what an idiot he was for giving Ray an out. He hoped he wouldn't take it and still answer some questions for him.

"No, it's fine, or we wouldn't be talking about it now. So really, what do you want to know?" Ray asked again.

Creed was thrilled and didn't know what he wanted to ask first. "Um, okay, well, did you pick up on any displays of odd behavior or weird habits he had?"

Ray giggled before he answered. "Creed, everyone is off to some degree or another, and everybody has odd behavior of some kind. It's what makes each of us different. It doesn't mean because you're strange that you'll turn out like that. But, no, if I ever saw any one thing that would pick him out as a serial murderer from the rest of the population, I'd say no, nothing."

"I always thought it would be something like that, something other people could pick up on. He was an animal, a vicious animal," Creed replied.

"You weren't planning on taking that test for detective, were you?" Ray asked, sounding concerned.

"Yeah, next year before the shooting happened, why?" Creed asked, curious as to what relevance that had to the conversation about Danny Rolling.

"Well then, maybe it's a blessing in disguise you don't serve anymore because you suck at it," Ray declared with a grin.

Creed was surprised Ray would say something like that to him, and he could tell he was going to need more time to adjust to Ray's unique personality.

"Yeah, thanks. What do you mean I suck at it?" Creed asked, slightly offended.

"Make no mistake, Creed, he was no animal. Animals kill because they have to survive, but humans kill because they want to. No, he was more like the proverbial 'monster in the closet,' lying in wait for just the right time to emerge and wreak havoc in the night. Yep, more like that," Ray explained.

"It's something in their brain, I think," Creed said.

"Oh, it's in their brain, all right. It's in everybody's brain. All of mankind is capable of such cruelties against other human beings. It's about choice, it's what we do with the freewill we have been granted. Each of us is responsible for doing good rather than evil with that freewill. There are some, like Danny and his kind, that choose to do evil, and there is no way to guess when someone is going to do harm with their own freewill, or even who they are. They hide in plain sight, that's why they're so damn hard to catch. He was no different than the rest of us, only his choices were different," Ray told him, and he thought Creed was getting it by the look of deep thought on his face.

"Yeah, I see where you're coming from," he replied. He thought Ray's view was bell ringing; it made perfect sense. Just as Ray thought, the resemblance Creed shared with Caroline was uncanny.

They arrived at the storehouse to find Mo putting some stock away. They all waved to each other, and Mo told the fellas to get what they needed, and she would mark it down. The two tended to their order pulling duties as they chatted about all the stuff that was there, most anything anyone could want. Much like a grocery store, Creed wandered each isle just to see all that was stored here and what wasn't. It seemed like everything he would need, so he didn't place a special order with Mo for anything, although he would like to get a bottle of whiskey since he was almost out. He hit two more isles when he happened upon the row of liquor. They had everything a package store would have, and he was impressed. He grabbed a bottle for himself and then another of brandy for Megan. He collected a few more items and took them to the front so they could be marked down for inventory purposes.

Ray finished his list, and then together they both gathered the things on Caroline's list. Creed was happy to help; he didn't have anything else to do but daydream about Megan. Besides, Caroline's list was for house supplies, so it was going to take a little while. Ray tore off the bottom of the list and gave it to Mo. It was a magazine list, and Mo always got them together for whoever it was to come get the list filled. Then he tore what was left of the list in half and handed it to Creed, and off they went in different directions to fulfill their duties of shopping for the house. It didn't take too long, and it was done twice as fast with both of them doing it. Mo got everything written done in her logbook and asked Ray if she could help him load it up. He declined, and the two loaded it themselves, while Mo went back to stocking a shelf.

As they got the last of it, Doc pulled up and got out of his jeep. They all shook hands and gave their greetings. Doc asked Ray how his thumb had been doing since it recently healed from being jammed from something stupid he was doing on his boat. Ray said it had been fine, and some other small talk was made. Then something in the air changed. It became heavy and still, like the planet stopped rotating, and the sea breeze that was a staple was now no more. The temperature seemed to rise a few degrees without the steady wind, and this time of year was too hot for that. Creed thought it was just him; he wasn't sure if Ray or Doc had noticed, and then Ray said it for him.

"Damn, you feel that, Doc?" Ray asked him as he looked up to the sky, and Creed felt better in a way that it wasn't just him. He wasn't losing his mind, not yet, since Ray noticed it too.

"Yeah, yeah, I do. Maybe you ought to go find Caroline," Doc told him. Both men were now looking up to the sky, and Creed didn't understand why. It was a perfect clear day, only suddenly now it was very hot.

"Yeah, I'm going. I gotta find out what's going on, and to make matters worse, I need to get this stuff unloaded before it rains," Ray said to Doc. Creed thought Ray didn't know what he was talking about. It was nice out, no rain in sight. No damn breeze either, and the air was getting thicker by the minute. Furthermore, he didn't know what Caroline had to do with the change in the atmosphere or why Ray needed to find her right away.

"Okay, talk to you later then," Doc said, and Ray said his good-byes. Creed waved bye, and they left, bound for the house. Ray drove a little faster this time, and before they made the first half mile, the sky drew dark. Huge gray clouds hung low, and Creed couldn't believe his eyes.

"How'd you know rain was coming?" Creed inquired of Ray.

"Because something is wrong, and I have to find Caroline," Ray answered.

"I'm confused. I'm talking about the rain coming, what's that got to do with Caroline?" Creed asked, clueless. "And what makes you think something is wrong anyway?"

"Because didn't you feel that? That change in the pressure? And the clouds moving in so fast is always a dead giveaway that something is amiss. That's how I know something is wrong with her," Ray explained.

"Actually, I did feel that. The wind stopped, but I don't get what that has to do with Caroline." Creed sounded even more confused than he already was.

"She brought the change. When something bad happens, this is what occurs. A storm brews, but first everything is still for a few minutes. Then the torrential downpour comes for how ever long the bad thing has a hold of her. The more upset she gets, the harder the rain comes down," Ray told him.

Creed thought for sure by the way Ray was talking he had burned up one too many brain cells with those lefties he smoked. He was just talking crazy now.

"Yeah, right, are you trying to tell me she's doing this because she's upset? That she can somehow control the weather? Give me a break," Creed said. He was thinking this was Ray's way of pulling his leg, a practical joke.

"I wouldn't say 'control the weather,' it's more like 'influences the weather.' After Carla died, she held it in for three days so the woods could burn, but when those three days were over, she brought a roaring tropical storm that subsequently put that inferno out. Thank God too because the smoke was so bad that even this far from it, we couldn't breathe," Ray explained.

"Man, c'mon, you know what you're telling me is an impossibility. People can't do that," Creed replied.

"You're right, people can't, but Caroline can." Ray tried to make him understand, but Creed didn't—not yet.

"How is that possible?" Creed asked.

"I don't know. How is anything here possible?" Ray replied. He wasn't able to explain it; it just was.

"Get outta here," Creed said as he laughed.

"Whatever. You'll see for yourself," Ray said.

They turned off the east road and was almost to the house when the rain started coming down in sheets. Ray pulled up close to the house, and the two men unloaded their booty as fast as they could. They threw it all on the back porch so they could sort it out of the rain. Gene saw them coming up the driveway and brought them towels to dry themselves with. Creed thanked her, and she went on about her business. When they ceased the water from dripping with the soft terrycloth towels, they were going to go to Caroline's office to see what was going on, but she stopped them in the kitchen. She entered from the hall, and they through the back door. Ray and Caroline stood and stared at one another for a moment until Ray spoke first. Caroline's eyes were swollen with tears, but she wouldn't let them flow.

"What is it? We were caught in the rain." He wanted to know.

"I'm sorry about that. Carl's dead," she said to Ray.

"Oh my God, Caroline, I'm so sorry. What happened?" Ray implored. Then he walked over to her and hugged her. Soaking wet, she didn't care; she welcomed his embrace.

Creed stood there feeling like the fifth wheel. He had no clue what she was talking about or who Carl was, so he thought he'd ask.

"Who's Carl?"

Caroline released Ray's hold and told him, "Carl is my younger brother, Carla's twin. He died this morning of an apparent overdose. He had a heroine problem he couldn't beat."

This made Creed mad in a way. She hadn't told him of a brother she had and why he wasn't living on the island with her. Maybe it was his habit or something else, but Creed had found out about him the hard way after he was dead. And why is it everyone associated with this place succumbs to a tragic demise? She needed to tell him everything, but now wasn't going to be the time.

"Why didn't you tell me about Carl?" Creed asked her.

"We just haven't got to it, that's all, and now's not the time," she said.

"What do you need me to do? Do you want me to take you?" Ray asked her.

"No, I'll be taking my boat. The rain will slack off some, I'll be fine. I'm going to go get his body. Gerald and Otis are already there, and I'll be back as soon as I can," she told him. "And, Ray, do me a favor, would ya? Can you give him some more family history lessons while I'm gone?"

"I sure can if you take the damn rain with ya when ya go," Ray answered, and a deal was struck.

"Done. Consider it gone," she said and turned to leave the kitchen.

"What the hell?" Creed asked. "What else do I not know?"

"There's a lot to know. You can't expect to get it all in less than a week. Pipe down. When she leaves, we'll talk, but right now, I'm gonna get out of these wet clothes and into a warm shower. You should do the same." Ray suggested.

Then Ray walked out and left Creed standing there alone with his thoughts. Disgusted with the whole Carl situation, the not knowing, Creed decided he'd open that bottle he just picked up and have a drink before and after that shower. All the information was making his brain ache; he'd have a couple of the baby blues to go with his whiskey. Times like this, they went well together.

For This Family Asunder Has Been Doomed

Creed caught back up with Ray a couple of hours later. After he had lunch in the kitchen with Bea and Gene, he found Ray in his office. This time, Herman Cain was talking on the radio turned down low. He couldn't quite make out what Herman was saying, but he was here for the radio talk show anyway. Ray offered him a drink, and he accepted, although early on, Creed had already started. The rain poured from the sky in buckets, and Creed thought it was a good time for one little jab.

"I thought she was going to take the rain with her," Creed said with his infamous tone of sarcasm.

"She will. She hasn't left yet. She had to get some things in order before she took off. See, come look. She's boarding her boat now," Ray told him, and then he got up and walked out on his back patio, and Creed followed him. Down at the dock, she was preparing to pull out, and the two watched her as she readied to go. After a couple of minutes, she pulled away from the dock and headed out to sea for the mainland. The farther away that she got, the less the rain fell. Creed couldn't believe it, thinking it had to be coincidence, which was a problem; he didn't believe in that. By the time Caroline was out of sight, the rain stopped completely, and the sun was out once again.

"See, told ya," Ray remarked as they both stared off into the distance.

"I don't believe it," Creed commented.

"Well, believe it. You just saw it with your own eyes," Ray said.

Creed didn't say anything; he just couldn't think the storm had anything to do with Caroline no matter how impeccable the timing coincided with her brother's, Creed's cousin's, death. No one has the power to control their surroundings like that.

"I know you don't believe me, but it's true. Ya know, when Luke died, it poured for a week. The trees couldn't take much more, and the ground was staying too wet for too long. I had to tell her she had to hold it back for a while. She was killing the grove, our income, with all that rain. She knew she was doing it, but controlling such feelings of hurt was always hard for her to do," Ray explained.

"I don't know what to believe these days," Creed said. He was throwing in the towel on this one. He didn't want to disagree all day over what he did see with his own eyes but saw in disbelief.

"Anyway, where should I start with trying to fill in the blanks for ya?" Ray asked. He wanted to tell Creed all he could so he wouldn't feel so out of the loop in the future.

"Well, you could start by telling me about Carl," Creed told him.

Ray leaned back in one of the rocking chairs on the patio and took a deep breath. Then he began to tell Creed all about him. Carl was troubled by the loss of his twin. He already had a few run-ins with the law, and it was a habit he couldn't shake. He tried rehab so many times—the facility needed a revolving door just for him—but to no avail. He never could kick it. When Carla died, as her twin, he felt it and hated himself for not being around when it happen. He wanted vengeance he would never get because he didn't get the chance. Carla was buried before the sun set on the same day it happened, and he couldn't get here until after her body was laid to rest. He never forgave himself for it, even though he couldn't do anything about it. He felt like he wasn't there enough for her and blamed himself for her death. Carl believed if he had been here on the island, Carla would still be alive. Although that couldn't have been further from the truth, he never got over it. After her service, Caroline tried to get Carl to stay here, but he would have no part of it. And the truth as to the real reason he wouldn't stay was because he couldn't get a fix here if he needed it. The dope man didn't deliver this far out. He'd have better luck ordering a pizza.

Ray went on to say that Carl wanted to do his own thing and have no part in following the family rules. Elliot Lenoit raised all of his children to be decent members of society, whether or not they walked on a good path was up to them, like a test. Carl couldn't be the son he should have been or abide by any set of rules, including the family rules. These, Ray explained, were supposed to keep everyone in line, therefore, setting the foundation for the next generation to keep the family and their own lives strongly together. However, Carl wasn't that kind; he was like a drifting free spirit, like his twin, but to a dangerous extreme, especially after that garbage took a hold of him and he lost the fight with his demons. Nobody could save Carl from himself, and the proof of that was in the manner of his death. Then when Carla died, it was all over for him. He was naturally closest with his twin, so her death was particularly hard for him. He never came back from it.

To add insult to injury, he thought he would inherit the island. Although Caroline was the older sibling, he was the only son, and he believed it was his birthright. Since he couldn't be decent, his father left it to Caroline instead. He was given a small monthly allotment, and that was it. It really burned him up, and Caroline even tried to compensate him with extra funds, but in retrospect, it probably only worsened his habit. The extra money more than likely just enabled him to have a larger habit. It was like pouring lighter fluid on a fire. Carl remained butthurt over it all these years and never got over it. Caroline visited him a few times, all of which went badly. Each time she would ask him to come home to the island, but he never would. It broke her heart every time she tried. Eventually, she gave up on her stalwart brother. She had this place to run and couldn't continue to try to babysit him from afar.

"And that's enough about Carl," Ray said.

"You told me she doesn't like to leave the island. Why didn't she have his body brought here? I mean, if all of my stuff can be delivered overnight, why not have him brought here so she wouldn't have to leave?" Creed asked.

"Because there's always what's left behind that needs tending. She'll go through his things and take anything important or sentimental and then have the rest of his belongings sent to a charity, all of which she prefers to do herself. She doesn't want anyone else going through his things," Ray explained.

"Yeah, that makes sense," Creed replied. He remembered how he had to go through his mother's things when she passed. He wouldn't have allowed anyone else to do it either. After a long silent pause, Creed had another question.

"Is that it on my cousins, or is there more I still don't know about?"

"Actually, there is one other, but Caroline may or may not speak of her. I suppose I should tell you, she did say to fill in the blanks for you," Ray informed him.

"Great, another one I don't know about," Creed said.

"And with good reason. Caroline's other sibling, Cora, would be the oldest of the four children. She was quite a bit older than the other kids," Ray said.

"Where's she? Why isn't she in the picture?"

"Caroline's daddy banished Cora from the family before Caroline went off to college. He not only denied Cora of her inheritance but he also went so far as to strip her of her name," Ray told him.

"What? Her name?" Creed asked. He didn't think someone could have their name taken from them.

"How can someone strip you of your name?"

"Because Elliot Lenoit could," Ray said.

"He had her named legally changed to Trinity May Smith. I never knew the man myself, and in a way I'm glad too because he scares the hell out of me, and he's dead," Ray said and did a little shake.

"Why did he change her name to that?" Creed asked. He didn't understand the reason behind having her name changed at all.

Ray laughed and said he asked Caroline the exact same question; it was like déjà vu. Then he began Cora's story. Apparently, she was a narcissistic royal pain in the ass. To hear Caroline tell it, Ray said Cora thought the moon and stars were hung just for her. And if one of those stars were out of place just a tad, the whole universe would have to stop to adjust its twinkle. She was way past selfish, and anything that didn't go her way was always everyone else's fault. She was controlling and manipulative to the point of pitting family against one another, creating drama every day. Her daddy tried to teach her to be nice and have compassion for others but not her hateful ass. He didn't understand it either. They raised them all with a lot of love and affectionate hugs; they hadn't been beaten or abused at all. Cora just had an evil streak four miles wide, and in old Elliot's mind, there was no reason for it.

So one day, Elliot brought her a little Collie mixed puppy, thinking it might soften her up some. Puppies have a way of lightening the heart and bringing joy where there was none, except Cora—she became angry that he didn't ask her what kind of puppy she wanted. She threw a temper tantrum like a child, and in the midst of her fit, she kicked the puppy in the head. When Elliot heard that little creature yelp out in pain, a whole different side of him came out that no one could've known was lying in wait. It was the first and only time he laid his hands on one of his children in anger. He slapped Cora to the ground and told her that was the last straw for her. He had warned her countless times to not be so nasty, but this time, there would be no warning—he was absolutely done with his oldest child and wanted her gone before she could poison the other children with her narcissism and foul behavior.

He made her pack herself a bag and then made her wait for him at the dock. Their mother had no problem with this due to all the trouble Cora constantly stirred. She had been sick of it for years and thought it was way past time for her to be booted out. She was grown and could take care of herself, so Elliot took her to the mainland where he arranged for her to be picked up and taken anywhere she wanted to go as long as it wasn't back to the island. The man who picked her up at the marina gave her an envelope with her new identification and ten thousand dollars. She was never to return. Cora didn't have to ask why she was given that name; she knew. Her father wanted her to never forget the Trinity—God the Father, Jesus Christ, and the Holy Spirit—that she didn't believe in. May was to remind her of when she lost her family and fortune, and Smith was to make her common, no longer a Lenoit. Her upper crust life was over as she knew it, and she would have to make her own way.

Cora hit rock-bottom in life, blew through the ten grand, and she couldn't hold a job because she simply thought she was above every job she had. She was too good and too pretty to have to work. She finally met her match when she started seeing a man whose ex-wife was just as pathetic and self-absorbed as she was. Only she was far nastier than Cora ever thought about being. When her new man decided he would mess around with them both, the ex couldn't take it, and when he said he wouldn't stop seeing Cora, the ex-wife caught up with Cora one night and cut her face up real bad with a box cutter. Cora was so ugly inside that she couldn't live with herself once she was disfigured. Not long after, she overdosed from the morphine pills she was saving up rather than take during her recovery. After her death, Elliot wouldn't allow Cora to be buried in the family plot, but he did pay for her services for her to be interred at the city cemetery. He considered her lucky to get that much out of him.

"Wow, that's crazy. So Elliot Lenoit was a hard man, huh?" Creed asked while he tried to digest Ray's information.

"From what I know about him, he wasn't. He was only hard when he was pushed to be, and Cora had pushed him the wrong way. But overall, I'd say no. Caroline speaks sweetly of him. She says he was a real good man."

"It sounds like they were a good family in spite of being slightly dysfunctional. But what family isn't anymore? I think the days of the Cleavers are over," Creed replied.

Ray nodded his head in agreement with Creed.

"Yep, for the most part. All families are screwed up to some degree. That's why I don't have any kids myself. I'd end up in prison for choking one of their little asses out," Ray told him and then laughed until he had tears in his eyes. Creed had to laugh too, for Ray was riotous when he was rolling from his own jokes.

"Caroline seems to like children, why didn't she have any?" Creed asked him.

"The truth is she tried, but she couldn't conceive. She thought it was her, so she had herself tested and found she was as fertile as the Napa Valley. It turned out that it was Luke that was completely sterile, and no doctor could explain why. Caroline decided that if she couldn't have Luke's children, she'd have no children, not even adoption," Ray explained.

"It was a blessing in disguise, really," Ray casually said, as if it were no big deal.

Creed thought that this is something you simply wouldn't say to the one affected by it. If this was Caroline closet relationship, a very long friendship, how could he say that?

"That's harsh. How is that a blessing?" Creed snapped in his asking.

"I'm not being ugly, I'm just saying, it's like…Okay, just follow me here for a minute. It's like the Lenoit name is cursed, the bloodline. Caroline is the last of the bloodline to have carried the name. She, we, believe the curse dies with her. In case you haven't noticed, everybody's dead. That's why she's tried to look out for you all these years. You're the only blood, distant or not, that didn't have the name. She knows you're safe, and you happen to be the only one left without the malediction."

"From the voodoo priest way back when?" Creed asked, his brow had come together from his deepened curiosity. He never believed in such things, but his mind was beginning to open up. Maybe everything wasn't black and white. Maybe there was a gray area and that the area was not only there but it was also vast. Maybe such things were possible in a place like this. It was very, very different here. There were so many maybes that spun inside his mind, and it was enough to give him a brain ache, which is a headache without the pounding throb.

"Ah, she told you about that, that's good. One less thing, ya know?" Ray said, happy to skip that. "But, yeah, that. She knows that's where the bad juju comes from, and she is, in a way, glad it will end, even if it ends with her."

"Yeah, right, I see. So that's it, there's no more family left?" Creed asked, making sure no one was missed. He really wasn't up for any more of those surprises.

"Nope, not now that Carl's gone. It's just you and her, but it wasn't like she could leave this place to him," Ray told him. Creed wasn't exactly sure what Ray was saying.

"What do you mean by 'leave this place to' precisely?" Creed asked. It would be best to stay on the same page and let nothing get lost in translation by trying to read between the lines instead of being direct and to the point. Brevity is always best.

"Just that who else is she going to leave it to? The island will be yours someday." Ray smiled as he spoke.

Hearing the words out loud seemed to sink in this time, and Creed could foresee all of this to be his one day. He didn't even know how to absorb it at all, but to hear him say it made it more real that it would be a reality one day. All of this was so unreal from where his life was not even a week ago. He couldn't quite grasp it all, and he knew it, but he was damn sure going to try. The island's dark past, the occasional creepiness up his spine, and dreaming about things he would rather not see were still better than a life of hiding and running.

"It's just hard to believe, that's all," Creed said.

"I know it is, but you'll get used to it. Is there anything else you'd like to know?" Ray asked him.

"Actually, I was at the cemetery with Caroline, and I saw some little wooden crosses around Luke's grave. I've been meaning to ask about them. Do you know?" Creed didn't know why he hadn't other than, like Caroline, he hadn't gotten around to it yet.

"That's Sully's doings, and Sully would be Doc. His real name is Brian Sullivan. Luke called him Sully, and they were very close friends. Doc liked to hear Bible stories, and Luke liked to hear surgery stories. It was almost comical when those two were together. Anyway, Doc whittles, he's the one that leaves those. I guess we all gotta have a hobby," Ray answered.

"There's something else I was wondering about. What did Caroline use as an accelerant to burn that fire so hot that nothing will ever grow back?" It was another thing he was curious to know but hadn't gotten around to finding out.

Ray blurted out a loud laugh and then said, "Creed, you wouldn't believe me if I told ya."

"Try me. Why wouldn't I believe you? Is it like some John Wick shit?" Creed said jokingly, and they both laughed a good bit. Then he realized something—he was comfortable enough around Ray that he could make a joke of something that he probably shouldn't with other people.

Ray let out another deep belly laugh and told him it was funny. He thought it was nice to know Creed was at ease to make wisecracks.

"All right, I'll tell you. Again follow me for a minute here. Just stay with me, even if it doesn't make sense to you." Ray insisted.

"Okay, let's hear it." Creed was all ears.

"It was her prayer. Her prayer is what made it burn like hell's fire. I swear to you it was. Just hear me out on this," he began to say. He knew that "get outta here" look on Creed's face because he saw this same expression on Caroline's face many times. "This is what happened," he continued.

Ray said that he and Caroline were together when she felt something. Something was very wrong, and she couldn't see it. What she could see was the thicket of woods that her intuition was leading her to. She grew up here and knew every inch of it, which was how she knew to go to that particular spot. Of course, he stayed with her to make sure everything was all right. She drove like a bat out of hell to get there, and when they did, she followed the impressions in the dirt, much like Leonard had. Ray didn't see Leonard or Billy hanging from that tree at first because he had been behind her as she led the way. She suddenly stopped when they reached the small clearing in the brush. He came around to her right and saw she was staring, so he followed her line of sight and saw him hanging there, gutted and mutilated. He couldn't believe his eyes, but it was real. He said he was so freaked out he froze for a few minutes. The words "Oh my God" were only mouthed because no sound would come out when he spoke.

Not Caroline, she fell to her knees and closed her eyes. She stretched her arms out with her palms up and began to pray. However, this was like no other prayer he heard her say before. He couldn't hear her words, but he could hear she was angry. He never heard her mad at God like that, and he thought if he were God, he would run as soon as he heard her coming. She never told Ray what she said during her prayer, and he never asked, but whatever it was, when she lit the small pile of dry sticks and weeds she had gathered, it went up like she had doused it with lighter fluid. He told Creed he hasn't ever seen anything like it, but he believed it was her prayer. Things happened when she prayed; it was like magic. It was not always, but sometimes it was pure magic. When Ray questioned her reasoning for burning it, she said she had no other choice. Billy's blood had been spilled there, and it was like poison. She had to burn it, burn the blood away.

Ray went on to tell Creed that Caroline wouldn't allow anyone to touch Carla's body but Doc, and that was only to embalm her. After Doc did his work on her, Caroline did the rest. She washed her sister's body and dressed her in Carla's favorite white gown. Caroline thought that not even death could steal her beauty. It pained her to prepare her little sister like this, but the responsibility fell upon her. They laid her to rest just before the sun fully set, and by then, smoke choked the island. By the time Caroline's rage hit its peak, the storm started and didn't stop. It was the worst week he could ever remember on the island. It went from bad to worse as time passed. At least, she relented with the rain before she killed the trees. She sent Leonard away the very same day.

Creed thanked Ray for telling him all that he had. It gave him more insight to the family, although torn apart and ripped at the seams, and of the island. The more he knew, the better, he thought.

"If there's anything I can do for you, just let me know. I appreciate all you've done for me," Creed said, hoping he could repay the favor someway.

"Well, there is something you could do," Ray said.

"Sure, name it," Creed replied, happy that there was something he could do to repay his kindness.

"Okay then, I was wondering how hard it was to deal with everything that happened after you shot that boy. I mean, it bothers you, right? If you don't want to answer, I understand," Ray asked of him. Creed thought about it for a second, and if that was all Ray would ask of it, it was the least he could do. Besides, he hadn't really talked about it, and it might do him some good.

"It's fine, I'll answer. Yes, it bothers me very much. I know I hurt his family. It hurt me too. A part of me died that day as well. I think about him and what happened every day. It's been the most difficult thing I've ever had to go through, and it ruined my life," Creed expressed.

"Did it really ruin your life?" Ray asked sincerely.

"Well, yeah, look at what I lost. My career is over. Life as I knew it is no more. Being a police officer is all I've ever known," Creed snapped at him.

"But look at all you've gained since. Look at how much more you stand to gain. It could have been so much worse." Ray reminded him. And he was right too. With all that had happened, he was very fortunate to be where he was and who he was with. For the first time, Creed really understood how lucky he was—not just lucky but also blessed. Then Ray reminded him of something else.

"Not to mention, Megan is digging on ya, and I know you gotta be liking that, my friend," Ray said, grinning. And he would be right about that too. He did like it, and he liked her.

"Speaking of which, I think I'll go look for her," Creed said, suddenly wanting to see her face and her smile.

"Yeah, you do that. I'll see ya in a little bit at dinner," Ray told him.

"Okay, see you then," he replied and left Ray's company to find Megan's instead.

Caroline arrived with Carl's remains before dawn the following morning, and Doc began the process of embalmment for the sunset burial. Afterward, his body rested in the island's tiny church until the time came for him to be interred. It had been Creed's first visit to the tiny sanctuary, and he found it to be as peaceful as the rest of the island. It sat off of the middle road, and its stained glass windows lit the inside of the church in a kaleidoscope of vibrant colors when the sunlight beamed through the colored panes. He pictured Luke at the pulpit giving his weekly sermons and wondered what worship was like in this house of the Lord. It was so small and quiet that he thought it to be the perfect place to come to pray and be alone with God. No one would hear his prayers here, even if he screamed them at the top of his lungs. He really liked the church and thought that the reason Caroline hadn't shown it to him yet was because she missed Luke so much that coming here would send her to the point of depression. He understood that, he often felt that same way when he would go to his mother's grave to clear off her headstone and leave fresh flowers.

No eulogy was given, and no words were spoken at his graveside. It was quiet and solemn, and everyone sat in silence until it was time for him to be covered with dirt in his final resting place. One more family member brought home, even if it was in a casket—Carl was home again. Caroline looked tired, and Creed could tell she had very little sleep, if any at all. He could see she was visually hurt, but he could also see she had a huge weight lifted from her shoulders too. Creed knew it was because Caroline wouldn't have to worry about her younger brother anymore; all his problems died with him. Creed thought about his own bad habit, and although he was glad his wasn't as severe as Carl's had been, he should work on getting rid of it. He saw it too many times when he was a police officer. When a person has a loved one with a bad habit, they always worry when that call will come, and when it does, they are left with only two things—one is the grief that is left in their troubled wake, the other is the relief that the call they always dreaded has come and that their worry for their loved one is gone and now a different emotion of sadness. That call is done, and the nightmare the habit caused is over. All that is left after that is moving on.

After it was over, everyone went back to the house and talked together into the late hours. Life would have to go on and continue as always. They all knew that days like this one are among the rest, and the curves life throws are meant for people to move with those curves and not to be knocked down by them. Carl's death would not stop the planet's rotation, and life would go on as it always did.

Too Often We Cannot See the Foretelling

As the next two years passed, changes for Creed came swiftly. Caroline had been correct in that he was, indeed, a wealthy man now. After his first harvest, he earned over sixteen million and tripled that the following year with Ray's knowledge of growing money into more money. Ray was truly talented at rubbing two pennies together to make a dime. The more Creed spread his wealth, the more it came back to him. He donated more than half of his money to the shelters the foundation built, and all he gave was returned tenfold. Caroline told him that this would happen because "you always get back what you give." The more time passed, the more blessed he had become. This too was something she said would happen, and in all the time gone by, Caroline had not been wrong about anything. He didn't always believe the things she said until they would come to pass, and then there would be no denying she knew what she was talking about. He would also discuss his dreams with her, and she would help him sort them out. There were several times when his dreams were actually predictions of the future he could not see. Caroline always sorted them out for him to understand and see them for the foretelling they really were.

In one of these dreams, he was holding a stack of old books that would have been impossible for any man to hold. The stack towered five feet above his head, and he walked among what seemed to be a thousand Haitians. As he stepped through the crowd, they would kneel and then disappear. They would say things to him in Creole, but there were so many, and they were all talking at once. He couldn't sort it out, even though he learned to speak the language. When he discussed it with her, she knew exactly what he was talking about, and she explained what it meant. Initially, she apologized that she hadn't shown him sooner, and then she led him to one of the cabinets in her spacious study. She pulled out books in twos until it was empty and stacked them on the floor, during which she said they were logbooks of all the slaves and freemen that ever worked for the family. Some had pictures, and others had descriptions of who they were and what their skills were. She told him he was welcome to look through them anytime, and when he took over, he would need to keep a written history like she did and all those before her.

He did ultimately study them in hopes that it would help connect him with the people who would eventually work for him. The more he read, the more he wished he could've done something for them. He discovered a couple of the early plantation owners were treating them horribly, and those that did suffered a terrible demise. Creed thought that although they were his ancestors, they deserved it.

He did find in the collection that there were some good ones that didn't view them as slaves but as the human beings that they were and they would provide very well for those who served them by the standards of the day. They were given more rations, clothing, land for their own food gardens, and other provisions that slaves were not allotted in other parts of the country. There was no need to whip them or mistreat them in any way because of two reasons—one being that it was an island and there was nowhere to run to, and the other was that most of the holders were decent, not seeing them as property but more like people who worked for what they were provided. Not every master was a tyrant and thought they were superior; some saw them as people with a funny accent and darker skin.

In those books, history had proven that kindness and tolerance for one another was always more profitable and effective than parochialism. Creed had the opinion that if everyone in the world would learn to coexist, it would be a near perfect world. But there was no such thing because bigots and zealots would always exist. It had been the nature of humans since the beginning of time to believe they are greater than other humans. Equality and good pay for the Haitians that worked here would be the only way to keep this island running like it needed to be, and that

Creed understood. Everyone here would have to work hard and do it together to make it work. And during harvest, it was hard work, and even harder to maintain the respect for others because when people are exhausted, the tempers can often flare quickly. He learned this through several situations that had occurred, but Creed was very good at defusing tension, and peace was kept during the season. His Creole came along nicely, and communicating became much simpler for him after his first experience with harvest time, and they respected him for taking to their language as well as he did.

Another of his dreams came to pass, which he didn't bother sharing with Caroline because he saw it as a sign. He dreamed Megan was in a simple white wedding dress with a crown of orange blossoms in her long braided blond hair, and she was walking toward him, smiling and with tears of joy welling in her perfect green eyes. He woke up with tears of his own and left that very day for the mainland to buy her the best diamond ring he could find. To his surprise, he found just what he was looking for at the first jeweler he went to. He saw this as a good omen too. He knew deep inside she would say yes because they really loved each other with all their heart. Although he wanted her more than anything in the world, he refused to deflower her before he felt it was right. In his mind, he thought that if she had kept her virginity for this long, he shouldn't take it until she was his in matrimony. And he didn't take it, even as much as they both wanted him to. There were times when it had been quite difficult not to, but she understood the importance of waiting.

Their wedding on the island had been beautiful and went off without a hitch. Although Caroline foresaw this too, she never mentioned her vision to either of them. She let it happen on their own time and without any of her coercion. She stayed out of their relationship because she knew it was none of her business; it was between them solely. Unless one of them was in some sort of danger, she wouldn't intervene. Caroline cried at their ceremony, as did everyone else. It wasn't every day that they had a life-changing event like this on the island, and they were all too happy to pitch in and make it happen. The late spring wedding allowed for excellent weather, and with all the gardens in bloom, the flowers were exactly how Megan imagined them to be. Even Mo and Doc helped Bea with the food preparation, while Gene decorated. A few of the Haitians came from the south end to bring benches and tables from the old chow hall. Everyone on the island attended that day, and celebrations carried on most of the night.

That night, he finally had Megan like he wanted to have her, and the two became one the way they both thought they would. He was more than pleased to lay his new bride down on what would now be their marital bed and take what had belonged only to her. He had never been with a virgin, and he was not disappointed with her lack of sexual knowledge. He knew that it would be to his advantage to teach her what she should know, the way he liked it. He also really liked the fact that no other man had her before him; it would be him and only him. He was afraid that since the first time hurts a little for a woman, she may not want to continue, or even bother, with lovemaking for a while. But that was not the case for Megan. It did hurt for a moment, but then it felt good. She was worried that her lack of skills may turn him off, so she was eager to please her new husband as best she could. However, Creed could never be turned off by her, even if she became disfigured and was covered in manure. He'd still want her after a shower, of course.

Their lives had been going well, except Caroline was spending more time with the ghosts she lived with. She had been going to the spring more often and sat on her wooden bench swing a lot more than usual. Creed brought the issue to Ray, but he told Creed to let it go. If it got worse, they would talk to her about it, but for now, they should just keep an eye on the situation. A few weeks after they talked, Caroline didn't show up for breakfast one morning. Everyone that lived in the house began looking for her, and they had Doc and Mo looking too. Three hours later, Creed found her in the church. She was on her knees in the middle of a prayer that she kept at a whisper. When she finished, she acknowledged Creed's presence and asked why he was there. He explained that everyone was worried about her, and she told him she had been there all night talking to Luke and God. Creed knew the emptiness since he passed was getting to her, but she would rather be alone than find someone else. No one would ever hold a candle to Luke, and Creed knew nothing he could say would bring her any satisfaction. He said nothing; he just knelt down on his knees beside her and stayed for a while. Sometimes the dead were better company than the living for her. For Creed, the dead would soon hold company with him as well.

One perfect summer morning, Creed had woken late. Megan let him sleep because he had been so busy helping everyone else during that period. After his morning routine, he went to the kitchen to grab some breakfast before he headed for the grove to pitch in. No one was in there, but Bea left a plate of freshly baked biscuits covered in plastic wrap on the counter. Creed took one and wrapped the plate up like it was. Her biscuits were the best, and after the first, he decided he'd have another. He had a couple of bites of it when he went through the back door to go see what was going on in the grove for the day. He was startled to see an old black woman sitting in one of the rocking chairs. Normally, the Haitians didn't do much work on this end of the island, but it wasn't unheard of either. He was surprised that no one told him that there would be anyone working at the house that day. He just assumed it was an oversight, and it really wasn't a big deal.

The old woman sat, rocking as she toiled at shucking a pile of white corn that was next to the rocker. A pile of husks and corn silk was on the other as she peeled it from the ears. Creed stood silent for a short moment before he spoke. He was trying to understand why the woman, in his opinion, was wearing such heavy clothing. It was so hot that summer, and the less, the better. She wore a long-sleeved simple cotton shirt with a long thick skirt and a half apron that went past her knees. She had a torn piece of fabric wrapped around her head tied in a four-corner style that made her look like an extremely aged Aunt Jamima. Her eyes were a cloudy cataract blue, and she smiled faintly. Creed nodded his head at her, and she stopped rocking as if she could see him through the clouds in her eyes. He thought for a moment he may have scared the near blind woman.

"Good morning. How are you today?" he asked the old woman. "My name's Creed." Then she began to rock in her chair again.

"I knows who you be, Massa," she said and laughed. "I's good."

"What? Oh, no, uh, I'm not a master. I don't know where you got that from, but those days are long gone. There's no master here anymore," he replied. He was stunned that anyone on the planet thought that way and thought she may have some dementia going on under her wrap.

"If you says so, sa," she told him as she carried on shucking her stack while she rocked.

"Yeah, I do say so. Please don't call me that. I'm just a man like any other. Besides, no one living today lives like that anymore," he commented.

"Yes, sa, if dat's whatchoo wants," she replied.

"Strange, I thought you'd speak Creole," he said. He thought everyone here was Creole speaking and was surprised she didn't have the accent. Hers was more Southern than anything else.

She laughed and said, "Nah, sa, I's bone in Joja. I's firs come here when I's foteen. I's always woked inda house doh."

Creed thought it was so odd that she was dressed the way she was, and she talked the way she did. He didn't think anyone was left in the world like that.

"I see. Looks like you got a lot of corn there to take care of. Can I help you with it?" he asked, thinking it would most likely take all day for the old woman to do it herself. Her hands were visibly arthritic, and he imagined her hands probably hurt like hell.

"Nah, sa, you gots anuff ta do wit dat seed, but you can have sommah dis if ya like," the old woman said as she handed him a cleaned ear. He popped the last bite of biscuit in his mouth and chewed as he took it. He did eat corn in the raw and wondered if she may have known that. He swallowed the last tasty bite of biscuit and then bit into the ear of corn. It was the sweetest he'd ever eaten, and he thanked her for it.

"No, I don't have any seed to take care of today. I don't actually do that. I do whatever is needed, but I don't exactly plant any seeds. Wow, this is really good corn," he remarked.

"Yes, sa, you plant dat seed all da time. It jus ain't took no root 'til now," she informed Creed.

He was beginning to think the old woman was in another world that was all her own, but he had a big heart for the elderly and had no intention of telling her how nutty he thought she was.

"Yeah, okay. Well, I'll leave you to it. I've got some things of my own to do. You have a good day, okay?" he said and took another bite from the sweet delicious ear.

"Yes, sa you do da same," she replied.

"Thanks again for the corn," Creed told her as he went out the screen door, shaking his head. He felt bad for the old woman being without a few of her marbles. He hoped he wouldn't become like that and wanted more than ever to be sharp as a tack when he reached his golden years.

Creed thought he would go check out the gardens while he finished his corn and was beginning to walk across the knoll toward them when he spotted Caroline and Ray coming back from the very place he was going. He wanted to apologize to them for oversleeping in case he may have missed anything important. It wasn't a normal thing for him to do, and he felt a little guilty that he wasn't up before everyone else like he usually was. Creed knew it really wasn't an issue, and seeing the two of them laughing as he headed their way was always good. He liked it when Caroline was smiling and happy, not sad or standing in that spring. Watching her out in the water motionless always made his skin crawl. He thought it was bizarre behavior, but he was not one to judge her for her actions when visiting whatever spirit she was in the company of at the time.

As the two approached, Creed noticed Caroline was looking at him in such a weird way; he didn't recognize what it meant. They all had just waved to each other, and suddenly she was giving him a funny look.

"Where did you get that?" Caroline asked as she pointed to the half-eaten ear he still held in his hand.

"Oh, this?" Creed answered and held it up.

"You should go get some. It's really good. I like mine fresh like this," he told her.

"Creed, there's no corn except for canned or frozen on the island right now. Where did you get that?" Caroline asked him.

"Sure there is. I'm eating it, aren't I? And I got it from the old lady that's shucking it," Creed explained. He couldn't understand what Caroline's problem was. It was just an ear of corn.

"The old woman on the back porch, she's got a whole mound of it she's been shucking," Creed told her and looked at Caroline, who was surprised; she didn't see the old woman earlier. The old woman had to have been there hard at her task for some time by the size of the pile she had already done when Creed ran into her.

"There's no woman like that here right now," she told him.

"Yes, there is. She's right up there." Creed insisted and pointed in the direction of the house.

"What did she look like, Creed?" Caroline inquired. She had no idea what he was talking about.

"Yeah, that's the weird part. She looks like she's real old timey by all the clothes she was wearing. Geez, it's hot. I thought everybody would be wearing cooler clothes right now, but not her. I'm roasting already myself," he replied.

Caroline and Ray turned to one another and gave each other a very puzzled look. Creed thought they must have left the house early, which was why they didn't know what he was talking about. Maybe they missed her because they weren't here when she showed up to take care of the corn.

"That sounds like Cibby, doesn't it?" she asked Ray.

"It does, it's gotta be. But why?" Ray asked.

"I haven't the foggiest idea, believe it or not. Let's go find out," Caroline said.

"Who's Cibby?" Creed asked. He didn't understand how neither of them knew she was there. They knew the coming and going of everyone on the island.

"I can't believe Cibby is up there. C'mon, let's go see what's going on," she told him. Then the three of them started toward the house. As they walked, Creed continued to ask who she was, but it was as though Caroline and Ray were in their own conversation and Creed didn't exist for the moment. It was a bit frustrating when it felt like he wasn't there. After a moment, Caroline turned to Creed without missing a step in her fast pace to the house.

"Creed, are you sure that's what you saw?" Caroline asked him.

"Yes, I'm sure. What the hell is the big deal, you guys?" Creed asked. He couldn't believe what an ordeal one ear of corn had caused. This was trivial, and Caroline was making it out to be an issue. The woman said she first came here as a teenager so many years ago, so Caroline had to know who she was. Maybe Caroline was confused when the woman would be scheduled to work at the house. Whatever it was, Caroline was certainly bothered by it.

"The big deal is no one is here that fits that description, and I want to know why. If it's Cibby, it's a good thing. She brings good news. She'll never tell of any misfortunes, always something good. Just seeing her is a good omen," Caroline explained.

The three reached the screen door and entered the back porch. Although it was the same one he exited, the woman wasn't there. Creed looked all around, bewildered by the old woman's absence. Not only was she gone but also both of the piles she'd been working on. Creed didn't understand; he couldn't believe it. There was nothing, not even a few missed hairs of the corn silk. It wasn't possible for her to have moved that pile of corn or cleaned up all the mess from it in the few minutes it had been since he left. He looked around, confused, having no explanation of what was going on, or in this case, what wasn't. The old woman had just been there. How could she have disappeared so quickly? Creed wondered for a moment if he was losing his mind. Was this place getting to him? Was he starting to crack up?

"I-I don't understand. She was just here, I swear." Creed pleaded. He knew neither of them would believe him. Caroline already expressed her doubt, but it was obvious she believed Creed saw something.

"I believe you, Creed, relax," she told him.

"Relax? How am I supposed to relax when I know good and well that woman was here. I'm still holding this ear of corn, for Christ's sake. How could it have not been real?" Creed declared.

"Oh, it was real, all right," Caroline said.

"What do you think her good news might've been?" Ray asked Caroline, now curious as to what old Cibby came to say.

"That's a good question. Did she say anything to you, Creed?" Caroline inquired.

"Um, yeah, but it didn't make any sense. She seemed to think I was a planter here or something—"

"A planter?" Caroline interrupted.

"Yeah, she said something about me taking care of the seed I planted. I tried to tell her I wasn't—"

"Oh my God!" Caroline blurted out.

"What? What is it?" Creed asked, almost startled by her reaction.

Caroline and Ray looked at each other as though they both knew, and Creed was odd man out again.

"Should I tell him?" she asked Ray. "Maybe it would be better if he found out on his own."

"Found out what? You know I really hate when you two do that. Now tell me what?" Creed demanded.

"Yes, Caroline, you should absolutely tell him. Don't leave him hanging like that, it's just wrong," Ray told her, and Creed was grateful Ray sided with him on it.

"Megan's pregnant. That's exactly what Cibby meant. But you didn't hear it from me, so when Megan tells you the news, you should probably act surprised," Caroline explained.

"Are you sure?" Creed asked.

"Without a doubt. I'm a hundred percent certain," Caroline told him.

"Wow," was all Creed could say as he took a seat in the wicker chair next to him.

Creed was happy by the announcement but shocked all the same. He was going to be a father, and he already knew he wanted to always be there for the coming child. He didn't have a father himself, but he would be diligent in being a good father. Then he began to get excited and wanted to go find Megan and tell her the good news. Caroline could read what was on his mind, and she told him. Although it was something good, he shouldn't take that away from Megan. She would be thrilled, and she would want to tell him, not him telling her before she knew herself. Caroline said that was just wrong to rain on her parade, and that it would be better if he waited for her to make the announcement herself.

He thought about it and agreed he wouldn't say anything, and he would act surprised when she told him. He sat in awe for a moment, and then the silence was broken when they both congratulated him. He smiled and said thank you when the kitchen door opened. It was Megan, and they all looked at each other, hoping she hadn't heard the conversation.

"Hey, honey, thank you for what? What's going on?" Megan asked with that sweet smile on her face he loved so much. He looked at her like he never had before. He couldn't believe that not only was he married to the most incredible, most beautiful woman in the world but that she also would bear his child.

"What? What is it, Creed? Thank you for what?" Megan asked him.

"Oh, I told him to take the day off today. He was thanking me, that's all." Caroline spoke up.

"Are you all right?" Megan asked lovingly.

"Yes, honey, I'm all right. I think maybe I just slept too much," Creed told his adoring wife. "Are you feeling all right? You're usually checking hives about this time of the day."

"Yeah, just a little nauseous. I think the heat's getting to me. I'm going to lie down for a while," she said.

Creed, Ray, and Caroline glanced at one another, and Creed asked her if he could get her anything. She declined and kissed him on his cheek before she went back inside for a nap. They all agreed that was a close one, and they didn't speak of it again until Megan rushed to Creed a couple of weeks later telling of the life inside her belly. She was so happy she cried those tears of joy for days. Creed picked her up and spun her around when he heard the news. He knew how much she liked it when he did that, and he spun her a few extra times. He told her how happy he was, and that made it even more exciting for her. All Creed wanted was for Megan to be happy, and pretending to be surprised wasn't that hard. Nothing was hard if it's what pleased her.

The following spring, their daughter was born. The moment Creed looked into his little girl's eyes, he knew she too had the gift. Even in her infancy, Creed could see that the perfect life he held in his hands could see too. Not like him, though, but like Caroline. The child had an "inner eye," which was far stronger than his gift of the dreams. The first time Caroline held her, she saw it too. She would stare deep into the newborn's eyes and smile because she knew she shared something special with the baby girl, something only the two of them would have. This child was special indeed.

Because What's Foretold
Is Blindingly Compelling

Caroline Carla Lowe was what Megan wanted to name the sweet child, and so it was. She was called Carrie for short. It didn't bother Creed in the least that Ruth wasn't a choice. After all, Ruth never wanted to have anything to do with the family anyway. What difference would it make? His little girl was perfect in every way—beautiful like her mama and sharp as a tack. She walked early, talked early, and had an uncanny quickness for learning. There was no doubt that she was as astute as she was cute in her little girl way. Creed loved his sweet daughter so much, and it was easy for him to understand the "Daddy's little girl" dynamic that fathers have with their daughters. It touches a man's heart to hear their little girl say, "I love you, Daddy." What father ever tires of that? None. Daddies love their little girls; they're sweet, perfect. Nothing feels better than when their little girl is holding their hand, and she looks up to her daddy with her sweet smile because she loves her daddy so much.

Sometimes he would look at her innocent face in amazement that he took part in her making. Perfection of life that she would come from his loins was, indeed, a blessed miracle. How could a creation of such divine giving have come from him? He would occasionally think of the way Elliot completely erased Cora from his life and everyone else for that matter. Creed couldn't understand how a father could dismiss his own child, going so far as to take her name. He didn't get it, but he also realized he wasn't in the situation to have to make that judgment, and he was damn grateful for it. He never wanted to experience that with the little girl that he loved so much. As a father, a daddy, he fully accepted that he was and always would be wrapped around her little finger. The most endearing words ever spoken were those four little ones, "I love you, Daddy." It's four taps on the heart every time she said it.

Creed would have a close relationship with her, and it stayed that way. Their bond grew tighter as Carrie grew older, always close with her father. She was just as close with her mother as well, and Megan was so proud of her daughter and loved her with all that she had. Megan would put Carrie's hair up every morning in whatever style the child so desired for the day—sometimes a ponytail, sometimes puppy ears or a head band with the rest of it down, and of course, the braid. A French braid was her favorite, and she wore her hair that way most of the time. It didn't matter how she wore it or if she were to go bald; she was cute as a button. She loved flowers like her mama and went to the gardens often to pick them. For a while, the child couldn't walk past a flower and not pick it. Eventually, Creed and Megan had to lecture the little girl to break her habit of picking every one.

Carrie had a close relationship with everyone who lived in the mammoth house in her own special way. She was always with someone doing something. She spent time with everybody and had a bubbly personality. She liked to watch Bea in the kitchen, and it always made her feel like a "big girl" when Bea let her help. Naturally, helping Bea make biscuits was her favorite. The flour and dough was fun, but cutting the big circles out that turned into biscuits in the oven was most fun of all for Carrie. She liked to color in her dozens of coloring books when she was with Gene, and she liked how Gene was so good at staying inside the lines with the crayons. Since Gene didn't speak and Carrie had her gift, she often knew what Gene was thinking, and they had their own way of communication. It was not quite like telepathy but more like a well-tuned in sense of what each was trying to express to the other. When they weren't coloring, they spent time in the gardens and picked fresh ones for the house arrangements or for themselves almost daily.

The child's bond with Caroline, her namesake, was especially close. Not only did they share the same gift but they also genuinely liked one another. Caroline would read to her and tell her Bible stories the way Luke used to tell Megan the Lord's tales when she was a child. They spent time together in the groves, and they too picked flowers as well. From time to time, Carrie would tell Caroline things that the little girl's "inner eye" would tell her, and each time it would come to pass just as the bright child said it would. She foretold of a coming summer that would be so hot; the fruit from the trees would be sweeter than they had ever been. She told of a death three days before it happened, a death of one of the Haitians on the south end. And she told Caroline about the deer that would come to her one day at the edge of the garden. She said that doe would let Caroline pet it and that it would follow her around for a while. About a week later, that too happened like everything the child said.

Things had been exceptionally good for Creed. He had everything he never thought he would— like the incredible bee charming wife that he had an outstanding relationship with. She truly was his best friend, and neither of them would ever give up on the other. They gave real meaning to what a spouse should be in every definition of the word. He had great and gifted children since Megan recently gave birth to their second child—a son who was named Lucas Patrick Lowe. The baby boy was called Luke, and Caroline cried, overjoyed by the honor of his naming. She thought it was a wonderful way to honor her beloved Luke. Caroline and Creed both knew right away that the infant was gifted as well, not like they were but like his mama. He too would one day be out in the groves enchanting the bees with his mother. Life here at the island had most certainly brought Creed more riches and enrichment than he could have ever imagined.

An added benefit was that Ray showed Creed how to turn his money over tenfold. He made some crucial investments and increased his wealth so high Creed couldn't give it away fast enough. Since he donated so much to the four homeless shelters, he was able to provide more services for them. He opened a clothes closet so they could get new shoes or a winter coat, and they provided any other articles of clothing they may need, undergarments to an extra blanket to keep them warm on the cold nights that winter brought. They also provided services for them such as drug rehabilitation, job placement for those interested in working or learning a trade, and educational classes from earning their high school diploma to college degrees if they so desired. It was his way of giving back to the community he left behind; helping from afar was better than not at all. He thought that it was the least he could do for all he had been given. He had overcome his demons of killing that kid, his feelings about his heritage, and, best of all, his addictions. He hadn't had a pill in nine years and rarely had a drink. Creed felt that helping others may help them overcome their demons as well.

With Ray's help, he had more than he felt he deserved, which was another reason he gave so much away. Along the path to his great wealth, Creed and Ray had become close friends. The friendship they grew to have also helped Creed understand Caroline a lot better. Ray knew her best, and he often explained to Creed why she did the things that she did, and why she was the way that she was. There were so many things he would have never understood about her had it not been for Ray's knowledge and insight. He appreciated having Ray around to tell him how things were when he had questions. Ray knew most everything there was to know about the island and the people who resided here, and his information was invaluable. He was very good at putting things in just the right order. Creed never thought he'd be such good friends with the fella he found to be so strange at first. But he was glad to know him and grateful for his friendship.

At Ray's urging and Caroline's permission, Creed pulled out all the old photo albums and journals kept from prior proprietors. After the incident with Cibby, they thought it would be in Creed's best interest to know who was who in case he had any more visitors in the future. He did his homework, and it paid off. It took months of study, thousands of pictures and pages he had to riffle through to learn all about the dead and gone, and even some of the living. Most of the records and catalogs were well kept, but others were in blotched and sporadic spurts for long periods of time. He found out that the old woman, Cibby, was a house servant, that she did come here when she was fourteen, and that she was born in Georgia like she had said. Cibby spent the rest of her life here, died here, and was buried here in 1858 at the very old age, for the time, of eighty-three. And the next time old Cibby came to see him, it was in a dream, and she foretold of his son's coming. When she came, he, at least, knew all he could about her. He didn't tell Megan. He let her have the bearing of good news all to herself again. No, he wouldn't take that from her this time either.

It was only about a year after Carl had died that Caroline opened the church for regular Sunday services. She had a big screen put up behind the pulpit to stream the weekly Sunday service by Pastor Michael Barnes that ran for the homebound members of the Church of Christ non-denominational fellowship or for those who wanted to catch it online. Brother Mike and Luke were good friends in the seminary days, and Caroline liked his preaching, so it only made sense to tune into him on Sunday mornings. Mike had even attended Luke and Caroline's wedding and said a few words at their reception. He liked Caroline and thought Luke had picked a fine woman to be his wife. Mike would kid Luke sometimes that he couldn't have done better than Caroline as his bride, and Luke always agreed. It was true—there was no better woman for him anywhere. Caroline liked Brother Mike too. She thought he was a good friend for Luke to have, both strong in their faith and like-minded on a lot of the same issues. So if they were going to watch anyone's sermon, it had to be Mike's.

All in all, Creed's life couldn't have been better. He even had his faith renewed as well as hope that the future would be just as promising. He had everything life had to offer, and he felt grateful to himself that he didn't pull the trigger that day in the hotel room. Life does go on, and one can only wait it out to see that. Creed had learned many lessons during his time here, all of which had their own significance, but one very important thing he learned was that there was great happiness in truth. The saying, "The truth will set you free," means so much more than by definition alone. Knowing the truth about any issue is workable. The truth can be dealt with and sorted through because it is the truth. Once it's accepted, one can move past it, and there is where the happiness will lie. Creed found that happy place when he accepted all the truth in the atrocities of the island and its people. He couldn't change the history here, but he could make it better by ensuring those things didn't happen in the future. A better place for everyone.

Luke hadn't been walking long when early one morning he wandered out of their wing and into the kitchen. The sun was still a couple of hours from waking at dawn, and Creed woke to use the bathroom. On his way back to bed, he looked in on the children as he always did, but on this morning, his son wasn't in his bed. Creed didn't wake

Megan; he went on the hunt for the little boy himself. He didn't think there was any reason to panic yet. He looked through the rest of their modified suite but didn't find him. He went down the hall and into the kitchen to find his little man on the counter with the plate of chocolate chip cookies Bea made the day before. Creed took two cookies and handed the boy one, and then he bit the other and covered the plate with its plastic wrap. He scooped the child up in his right arm and adjusted him onto his hip. On his way back down through the hall, he looked out toward the shoals and noticed Caroline sitting on the swing in the dark by herself lit only by the moon. He carried Luke back to his white with red racing stripes racecar bed as the little boy finished his treat and then laid him down and covered him up. After that, he went out to check on Caroline.

She was gently swinging when he sat beside her, and then together they fell back in sync with the easy rhythm. He asked if she was all right, and she told him she couldn't sleep. She had some of those nights, and it had been one of them. He had one of those occasionally himself, so he understood that. They sat quietly for a few minutes when Creed felt compelled to say something.

"Caroline, I want you to know how grateful I am for all you've done for me over the years. I wouldn't have what I have or be who I am today if not for you. Thank you and I really appreciate everything," he said, happy he got that off his chest. He couldn't remember the last time he had told her that, and he felt it needed to be said.

The corners of Caroline's mouth turned up to a soft smile as she continued the even swaying of the swing.

"I know you do, Creed, and you're welcome. But there really is no need to thank me. Everything was by your own submission, not mine," she replied.

Creed wasn't quite sure what she meant. He thought about it for a minute, but he still wasn't sure. He had learned that if he didn't understand exactly what she meant by something, he should ask for an explanation because chances were his interpretation wasn't at all what she meant. That had happened too many times before.

"By my own submission?" he asked her.

"Yeah, by your own submission. What we submit to dictates who we are," she told him.

"I'm not sure I follow. What do you mean?" Creed asked her, increasingly puzzled by Caroline's words.

"We all submit to something. Luke submitted to his faith in the Lord, Carl submitted to the heroin, Ray submitted to his inner self. It's all of us. We become what we create of ourselves by the things we choose to submit to," she explained.

Creed bounced that around inside his head for a minute, and her perception on that made a lot of sense to him. She was so good at that, and she was always right about her take on something. Then he had another question that needed an answer.

"What did you submit to?" Creed asked her.

"Me? This place…this family. It's who I chose to be and what I chose to have," Caroline answered.

Creed thought she hit the nail on the head in her statement. It was true, that's exactly what she submitted to, although he thought she left out the part of living with the ghosts. Then he thought about himself. He wondered what her thoughts were of what he chose to give himself to.

"And me? What do you think I submitted to?" Creed asked. He couldn't wait to hear her assessment of him.

"You submitted to a plan that wasn't your own. The plans you had for yourself aren't at all the plans you follow now. You thought being a hotshot detective was what you wanted for yourself, but it's not. And you're happier if you think about it," she explained to him.

Caroline was right—he didn't have to think about it; he was happy. And, no, it had not been his plan at all that he would be working and living on such a beautiful island or being married with children and wealthy beyond measure. But it was true in the words she spoke—he couldn't be any happier, even if it wasn't his plan. His plan was to be a detective and one day retire from the force, but that boy he killed wasn't part of his plan and because of it, his plans changed. He considered what Caroline said, and maybe what he was doing with his life wasn't what he counted on.

But truth was spoken of his happiness, and as bad as it was in what had happened to cause the change, he was grateful for it.

"You're right. I am happier than I ever thought I would be. It's strange the things we think will make us happy in life, and then something happens that brings better things we didn't expect. But you're absolutely right, I didn't plan any of this, and I wouldn't trade any of it for anything in the world." He agreed.

"I'm with ya, me either," she told him.

"Submission, huh?" he asked. "I never really thought about it like that."

"Yeah, but when you do, it makes sense, doesn't it?" Caroline stated more than she asked.

"Yeah, actually it makes perfect sense. But then you're good at making sense of just about anything," he told her with a slight grin.

Caroline laughed out loud. "I don't know about anything, but I try."

They continued to swing and talk until the sun woke. As it rose, Megan brought them both a cup of coffee and left them to their time alone. She knew it was always good for her husband to sit and talk with Caroline. He always came away from a conversation with a better understanding of whatever it was they would discuss. He would come away with newfound knowledge, even if they just sat and didn't talk at all. Creed had come a long way since he first stepped foot on this island. He was a deeper man but still hard when he needed to be and each time becoming a little less hard. A hard ass wasn't what he wanted to be and chose not to, submitting to being a kinder man, a decent human in which there were so few left in the world. He hoped that nothing happened on his watch that would force him to make justice come swift like the times before he came here. If he ever had to be judge, jury, and executioner, he'd like to be decent about it and not have to kill anybody.

The next morning was a glorious Sunday, and as usual, everyone had been at the small church for the weekly morning service—everyone except Caroline. Although she never missed a sermon, it was no surprise, considering she had complained the previous evening of a screaming headache. She had taken some ibuprofen and turned in early, so her absence was understandable. Creed thought he'd remind her that she could watch the service at a later time by logging onto the church's web site. It was awesome preaching by Pastor Mike about giving all your troubles to God and about loving one another as Jesus loves us. Creed knew Caroline would love this sermon, and he wished she hadn't missed it. He decided afterward he'd ask Doc to come see her later that morning if her headache hadn't gone away.

When it was over and Creed was talking to Ray for a few minutes, Carrie ran up and tugged on her daddy's pant leg.

"Daddy, daddy, can I go pick flowers with Bea before lunch? Please, oh, please, oh, please, can I?" The little girl shrilled with excitement, unable to contain it.

"Yes, sweet pea, of course, you can," he told his adoring daughter with a very proud smile.

"Oh, thank you, Daddy." Then she hugged his leg and skipped her way to where Bea had been standing, talking with Megan. Ray and Creed departed so Ray could get a sandwich, and then Creed went over to his wife, holding their son. She mentioned she wanted to check some honey samples she had taken the day before, and she would take Luke with her. He agreed and kissed his wife and son good-bye until lunch when they would meet again. Megan strapped the small boy into the child seat in her jeep and then buckled in herself and waved as she drove away. With Ray gone already and Megan too, he had no ride back to the house, so he caught Bea just as she was pulling away in the golf cart she preferred as transportation. She gladly told him to hop on; she had to go past the house to get to the gardens anyway.

As he rode on the back, he enjoyed the backward view the cart provided. He was getting a bit choked up listening to his little girl giggle and chatter on about all the different flowers she wanted to cut. She would name which flowers she would select for which rooms she wanted to put them in. Her room naturally was on her list. Creed secretly thanked whatever divine power that was over him for that very moment to hear his sweet Carrie go on like the chatterbox she was being. She couldn't have been more precious in her sweet innocence at that moment. This memory, like so many others, would be etched in his mind for the rest of his life, and he'd never forget this one.

Bea pulled up to the back of the house near the kitchen to let Creed off. He stepped down and leaned into the front to kiss his daughter's cheek. She giggled and smiled at him, and his heart was filled with love for her. He said good-bye to her, and as Bea began pulling away, Carrie turned back to Creed to wave.

Then she said, "You should check on Auntie." Her smile was bright, but her message was haunting. Creed's happy grin turned to a fast frown. He had to think about what she told him to do. *Is that what she said?* he wondered. Why would the little girl so eager to get her flowers say such a thing? He had that confused puzzled look on his face, the one where his brow comes together in a crease between his eyebrows. Creed was well aware of the child's intuition, but this statement from the mouth of his babe was chilling, almost scaring him. That infamous creep crept up his spine until every hair on the back of his neck was standing up. The look in Carrie's eyes was seriously deep as she said it again.

"You should do it soon, Daddy. "Although Carrie wasn't upset in saying it, the way she looked at him and the way she said it was very unnerving for him. Bea drove away as though she hadn't heard the little girl.

The moment Carrie was no longer looking back at him and turned around in her seat, facing forward again, Creed raced to Caroline's suite to do the task his little girl suggested. He was struck with panic, suddenly worried because the suggestion came from Carrie, and her insight was special, like she knew something no one else knew. Creed sprinted down the corridor that lead to Caroline's suite and found her door wide open. He slowly looked inside and saw Ray on his knees beside her bed holding Caroline's hand as the tears fell from his eyes. He was seeing it but wasn't believing it. It couldn't be…it was only a headache. How was it she lay lifeless? Creed felt a sharp stab in his gut. Of all he saw while he was on the force, he could've never prepared himself for this. But he knew the look of death when he saw it, and he knew immediately death had come to her. His heart sank, and he suppressed the urge to vomit. This couldn't be happening to him, not now. She was only in her mid-fifties, and she was too young to not wake up.

Creed went to Ray's side and knelt beside him as his own tears began to fall. In her white cotton nightgown, she looked completely at peace and no longer looked tired like she had been for sometime now. Creed took Ray's hand that held Caroline's and enveloped them with his own. His heart was breaking at both the hurt he felt and the hurt he knew Ray was feeling. Their friendship spanned decades, and this loss would be the worst Ray had ever experienced.

It would be especially difficult for Creed, who had her as his sole relative and now gone for reasons no one could've foreseen. Creed agonized over how he would do any of this without her. He needed her, and clearly she had passed a few hours ago. There was no saving her or bringing her back; she was gone. Neither of them left her side until Doc came in about fifteen minutes after Creed. Doc thought he would go ahead and look in on her instead of waiting until later as Creed had asked him after service. Not that it would have mattered; there was no hope for her.

The three bowed their heads, and Ray prayed. After his prayer was finished, Doc checked her out but had no definitive answer for the cause of her untimely and unforeseen death. But Creed knew she died from a broken heart no matter what Doc had said. The news of her passing traveled fast, and everyone funneled their way back to the house. Everyone, overwhelmed by the loss that was felt, couldn't stop the tears—all but Carrie, that is. Although the mood was sorrowful and dark, she didn't shed a single tear. The child could only say that Auntie was happy now, and she was with the people she loved and missed. The young girl's perception was something altogether different from any Creed knew of. But she had a good handle on things, and one can't argue that when their understanding of particular situations is far deeper than another's. All he could do as her father was accept that that was how she saw it.

Caroline's body was given the same care as any other. Doc embalmed her like he had done for some many of the other family members, and then Megan washed her and dressed her. She too would lie in the church waiting for her sunset interment while everyone said their good-byes to her. In the church, Creed stood with a numbing pain of deadness not only in his heart but also in his soul. He was just talking to her the night before and tonight she would be in the ground. In a matter of hours, she was gone forever. He would never hear her words of wisdom again. He thought about how fast life moves sometimes. In a moment, it can be all over, and the rip inside is excruciating. After Caroline was covered with the last of the dirt for her grave, Doc placed a wooden cross he had whittled on the fresh soil and then placed one at his old friend Luke's grave, which was next to hers.

Within the next three days, all her assets were inherited by Creed, and Ray was finished with all the paperwork. The increased wealth and ownership of the island didn't make him feel any better. He would've rather had Caroline around instead. None of it meant anything without her. The days that followed were no better. After seven weeks without Caroline and without any rain, the trees weren't taking too well to the drought they were having. The spring just couldn't supply the entire grove without the occasional downpour. Creed was discussing what their options were with Ray. Since they were to lose a lot of fruit from it, they needed to come up with something and fast. Then Carrie came in on their conversation when she brought them fresh baked cookies, which she helped Bea make, for them to try.

"Will the trees die, Daddy?" she asked in that innocent tone of hers.

"Well, baby, they might. The trees need the rain, and so do your flowers that you like to pick so much," he answered her.

Then without warning, she threw them both for a loop.

"Do you need me to make it rain, Daddy?" she asked, as if this was common.

Creed gained his puzzled face and Ray his surprised look. They glanced at each other and then back at Carrie. Neither of them could believe what they had just heard.

"Can you do that, sweet pea? Can you make it rain?" He almost couldn't believe the words that had just come out of his mouth. Did he really ask his daughter to make it rain?

"I can, but I thought the rain would make you sad, and you've already been sad. I didn't want you to be more sad," she said sweetly.

Creed was overcome with his child's concern for him. He had to expect that she could sense how he had been down in the dumps since Caroline died. But what he hadn't expected was that she too, like Caroline, was a rainmaker.

"If you can make it rain, that would make Daddy happy. If it rains, I promise I won't be sad anymore. The rain would make me feel much better," he explained to her.

He wondered how he had no knowledge of her ability to make that happen. Then he wondered if she did make it rain, would that be exploiting her? He thought for the sake of the trees it would be worth it.

Carrie smiled at Creed, and then thunder clapped overhead. Creed and Ray looked at each other in amazement, and then it roared louder. She handed them each a cookie, and before she could finish the one she took for herself, a torrential downpour had begun. The monsoon was raging when Creed snatched her up and ran outside with his daughter and danced as he laughed in the much overdue rainstorm. He laughed until he cried as he twirled her around. He told her it was a good thing she was doing— making the rain. The trees would make it after all.

Epilogue

I swayed in Caroline's swing in the same slow rhythm she did. For whatever reason, it made me feel a little closer to her. I tried to do a lot of things in the same way she did—not everything, though, but a lot. I kept the journals up to date, and there wasn't a decision I made without considering what her solution may have been first. Some things I talked out with Ray or Megan, but some things I made an immediate decision about without anyone's input. Today I'd make no decisions, for my thoughts were with her mostly. I really missed her, and she had no way of knowing how much I needed her. I told her, but who knew when she was listening, watching. I like to believe she checks in on us, but that too could just be wishful thinking. I would do almost anything to hear one of her stories, to hear her voice, to feel her living, breathing presence beside me on this swing. I only had memories of her now, memories and her reflection that stared back at me every morning in the mirror—same eyes, same hair, same features, and almost the same laugh. I couldn't look at myself anymore without thinking of her and of how much I missed her.

There is a hawk that comes each morning I come out here and sit. It sits in the lower branches of the trees across the way and watches me. I watch it too. When it cries out, I am moved, and I'm not sure why. I could only guess it is because God granted me this moment to be in its company, like when I was granted the time I shared in Caroline's company. Every time was a blessed moment given by God. I didn't fully understand what she meant at first when she told me I'd followed a plan that was not of my own. She said the reason for all my underserved rewards was because I followed a higher agenda that was not my own. I looked at my loved ones and all that I had, none of which was in my design, and I knew what a fortunate man I was to have been brought here in the lowest point in my life. I also knew that I was lucky for the bad luck I had at the time. Had it not been for the bad luck, the good luck wouldn't have come. All because I did something caused by forced change that led me down a path I wouldn't have chosen of my own volition. Yet here I sat with the hawk, king of my world. It could only be due to something higher than me.

It seemed as though that curse Caroline believed in did die with her like she thought it would. For the most part, all had been good here. There were a few bumps along the way, but that was just par for the course. Other than the one major incident, there had been no trouble to speak of. It was near anarchy, and I wasn't sure it would turn out like it did. Learning Haitian Creole paid off during the time because communication was the only way to resolution in the matter—just one more thing Caroline was right about. It sounded one way to us in our language and sounded like something altogether different in theirs. When it could be looked at in two different ways, then somewhere in the middle it was seen for what the matter really is, like two sides to every story, and somewhere between them is the truth.

Phillip did bring it to my attention; however, he thought it was settled. It was a dispute over a goat of all things. Two of the other permanent hands, Yann and Frantz, had some disagreements over Yann's pet goat, which constantly wrecked Frantz's food garden. Yann, in no way, tried to remedy the problem; he continued to allow the goat to roam freely. Then supposedly, Yann fell from the roof while making a repair. This, however, wasn't exactly what everyone else thought had happened. Because of the ongoing dispute, most of the permanent Haitians believed Yann was pushed. Not to mention, when Doc examined his body, he had an unexplained head wound, which split his skull nearly six inches. It wasn't caused by the fall; clearly, he'd been hit before he left the roof. There were no witnesses to it, but it was obvious. When it reached the point that we now had a dead man, it was no longer Phillip's problem; it was mine.

I remembered something Caroline had said once. She said, "Sometimes, heaven and hell are the very same thing," and at the time of that crisis, I understood exactly what she meant. My heaven had become my hell in a snap. It was up to me to make that decision, and I needed Caroline's advice more than ever. Without her, I made it on my own, seeking no suggestions from anyone. Neither did I think I would've listened to anyone if they had any. I had to make the best decision for the kingdom as a whole, not what anyone wanted me to do. I immediately brought Frantz to the house for his safety until I decided what to do with him. Those that thought him to be guilty wanted their own retribution. But I had learned something about retribution—it was served harshly, and the punishment almost always far exceeded the crime. And I decided there had been enough killing over the years in the name of justice. Justice here on this island with these people wasn't served as justice but more like retribution. We were done with that; change had come.

The decision I made was to remove Frantz from the island and send him back to Haiti. Although I knew how Frantz felt having everyone after him, I couldn't sympathize, considering the reason behind his actions. Ray and I arranged his departure and had him off the island within a half hour of bringing him to the house. It was, in my opinion, the best decision for everyone involved. An hour later, I had twenty Haitians from the south end marching up the drive. The uprising called for Frantz, and when I explained to them in their own language that I had sent him away, near mutiny broke out. They were angered, but all the murderousness of the past was in the past, and I would do things differently than they had been done before. Bloodshed would be no more if I could help it. We would live in peace here. I went on to tell them I would hear no more of it, but I had sent him to his hometown in Haiti and that if something did happen to Frantz, it would be there and away from Twisted Oaks.

I believed what Caroline told me about freewill and karma going hand in hand. I had freewill to do what's right, and in doing so, I hoped the karma kept coming for it. That was my submission—do what's right, even if it's not my own plan, and the rest will follow because it wasn't what I wanted to do, but it was the right thing to do. I couldn't feed Frantz to those wolves, for the wolves will be back for me. My reckoning was foretold by another, and in it I stood. This was what I chose. A long time ago, Caroline asked if I knew why I was named Creed. When I told her I didn't, she smiled softly and told me it was because my mother wanted me to be better than my father or any other man she'd known, live by my own creed, and to be a good man with genuine empathy for other human beings. She hoped my convictions and my beliefs would be better than most. I liked to believe mama can see me and know I turned out better, even in a place she hated so much. I hoped Caroline was happy too; I envisioned her with her beloved Luke.

I should go inside, but I don't want to leave this spot or my thoughts of my cousin, Caroline. The hawk called out, and it sounded like it was crying, like the way my soul felt without her. It's true what she said, that paradise and purgatory, like heaven and hell, are often the very same thing. I think I will stay just a while longer.

CPSIA information can be obtained
at www.ICGtesting.com
Printed in the USA
LVOW12s0004160916
504815LV00013B/54/P